HEART
OF
FATE

CONNOR WHITELEY

DEDICATION

Thank you to all my readers without you I couldn't do what I love.

CHAPTER 1

Smelling the rich fruity sweet breads, Alessandria had to smile as she looked at the impressive array of loaves in all their different shapes and sizes on the wooden market stall.

Picking up a bright yellow spiced loaf, Alessandria was surprised that the leaf was so soft like a pillow. Maybe this would be a good loaf for the wedding.

The sounds of people talking around her made Alessandria remember that she was in the busy market. But when she was with all the beautiful bread, why would she want to remember?

Turning around Alessandria frowned at all the people in the market. Some were innocently shopping and exchanging coins with the other stalls that were arranged into neat little rows upon rows.

But other people were shouting and mocking others as they walked.

If the market was on her Family's land, Alessandria would arrest them all or at least get them to move on quickly. This was a market, not a pub.

A part of Alessandria wished her beautiful Nemesio was here. If nothing else, she could admire his perfect hair and his beautiful movements. In practical terms, there's nothing like a Former Inquisitor to strike fear into the hearts of those shouting at people. For Inquisitors might all be so-called powerful arrogant zealots but they have their uses.

Looking around for Hellen's massive wooden stick and her typical grey Procurator cloak, Alessandria saw all sorts of people doing their morning shopping in the cool early autumn air. But still no Hellen.

Turning her attention back to the loaf in her hand, Alessandria thought about if this would be a good addition to the wedding. The Queen's staff was doing the cooking so this loaf would be rather pointless next to those towering creations. Yet it was always the thought that counted, at least that's what her Father use to say.

Passing the money over to the man behind the stall, he gently wrapped up the loaf in rough cool brown paper and Alessandria placed it in her black leather bag.

The sound of wood hitting the cobblestone ground made Alessandria smile and turn to face Hellen as she wandered over. Her grey Procurator cloaked having spots of mud on the bottom from the summer before. Alessandria really wanted to make Hellen wash the cloak. Was that rude?

"Look at those thugs. What ya think?" Hellen asked.

Alessandria's eyes narrowed at the group of men and women around the edges of the market. There were definitely more of them now.

"I think they look like Church peeps," Hellen said.

Alessandria still didn't say anything, but Hellen might have a point. The fact that the church were being more vocal as the wedding came closer hadn't escaped her notice. Nor did the increasing attacks being committed by church people.

"Did ya buy anything nice? I bought Daniel and Harrison a nice marital aid,"

Alessandria just looked at Hellen. She opened her mouth but closed it.

Hellen nodded. "They're gonna to love it,"

Alessandria wished the ground would swallow her up. She was definitely going to miss her friend when she was gone.

The group was getting louder. Their shouts were getting easier to hear. Something about stop the abominable marriage.

As much as Alessandria wanted to march over there and explain that two men getting married was fine and it wasn't causing anyone any harm. She knew better than that. She had tried it hundreds of times before. It always ended badly.

"Should na we go?" Hellen asked.

Alessandria knew Hellen was right. They did have other things to do and for some reason Hellen wanted to go dress shopping for the wedding.

But a part of Alessandria wanted to stay. She needed to protect these innocents in case something happened.

Alessandria nodded. "You're right. Let's go and-"

Bottles smashed.

people screamed.

Fire engulfed market stalls.

Alessandria whipped out her sword.

The group advanced.

It was a mob.

Men and women screamed scripture and anti-gay words.

They destroyed market stalls.

Smashing fists into people.

Alessandria needed to act.

Hellen surged forward.

She whacked some people with her stick.

Bones crushed.

Muscles snapped.

Alessandria joined.

She stormed forward.

She swung her sword.

Slashing and lashing at the men and women.

Blood sprayed over the cobblestones.

Blood covered Alessandria's armour.

More mobsters attacked.

Smashing their fists into Alessandria.

The bread loaf got squashed.

Alessandria's blood boiled.

How dare they!

Alessandria slashed the heads off her foes.

Heads rolled.

Corpses slumped to the ground.

The fire roared.

Spreading through the market.

Flames licked Alessandria's arms.

She needed to move.

Alessandria charged out the market.

She couldn't see Hellen.

The sound of whacking and shattering skulls caught her attention.

Hellen was still in the market.

Horns echoed in the distance.

The army was coming.

Flames turned the market to ash.

The fire roared.

It was getting closer to Hellen.

Hellen hadn't seen the flames.

Alessandria charged into the flames.

Leaping over flaming stalls and smouldering corpses.

She reached Hellen.

Alessandria slashed the back of one man.

She grabbed Hellen.

They charged out of the flames.

Alessandria turned to her.

Flames engulfed Hellen's cloak.

Alessandria looked around.

There was no water.

She turned back to Hellen.

Hellen was already rolling around on the ground.

She was thankfully safe.

Allowing herself to take a long deep smoke-filled breath, Alessandria looked at the smouldering ruins of the former market. Great columns of black smoke raised up into the sky. Corpses smouldered.

All whilst the remaining attackers ran away. They would most certainly pay for their crimes.

When Hellen got up, Alessandria hugged her. She wasn't ready to lose her yet. After the smell of Hellen's smoky cloak was too much, Alessandria pulled away.

She was about to go and grab a horse from a nearby stable when the deafening sound of tens of horses flooded the market square. The horses pounded into the cobblestone.

Once the horses surrounded the market and started to interrogate people. A large black horse came over to Alessandria and Hellen.

Looking up to the rider, Alessandria was more than happy to see who it was. Admiring that beautiful red and blue fiery armour and that wonderful long hair, Alessandria gave her perfect Nemesio a hand down from his horse.

She gave him a kiss.

"Why ya looking so down?" Hellen asked.

Alessandria looked at Nemesio. Her friend was right, he was frowning- a lot.

"Alessandria, you need to come back to the castle," Nemesio said.

"Sorry but I need to-"

Nemesio cupped her face in his big strong hands.

"Alessandria, I'm sorry. Your Mother is dead,"

CHAPTER 2

Considering I rarely feel too much emotion, I have to say I'm loving this wedding prep!

Even now as I spun my dulled blade slowly in my hand and look at the amazing decorations in the Royal Hall with the diamonds pressed into the walls, the massive sheets of white golden silk hanging down and the gold leavened marble floor. This was amazing!

I didn't even care that the silk sheets smelt of overpowering sweet blood oranges, cedarwood and sea salt. They looked great. But the delicious taste of orange drizzle cake filled my mouth. Maybe I would sneak down to the kitchen later and grab some. You know quality assurance and all that.

Even at the very end of the halls tens of metres away, the raised platform (where I'll be married to the love of my life!) was decorated with gold and rubies and pearls. This was going to be stunning!

The sound of my beautiful Harrison coughing in his smooth wooden wheelchair made me look down and kiss him on the head. His soft longish blond hair felt great as I ran my fingers through it.

Harrison tilted his head back to look up at me. He too couldn't stop smiling. This was actually happening. We were really going to get married.

I gave him another kiss before I let go of the wheelchair and Harrison rolled himself away. Just watching him was a gift in itself. Watching my perfect paralysed boyfriend being happy and accept what happened to him was good.

Of course it was hard for both of us at first, Harrison wasn't exactly nice to me as I tried to help him but I stayed. I protected him and I helped him because that's what you do for the people you love.

I'm glad I did stay and help him because if I didn't then I wouldn't be able to admire him now as he rolled himself around. His strong arms pushing those wheels. It was a rather good sight.

The massive wooden doors swung open.

I whipped out my sword.

Harrison rolled over.

Alessandria stormed in.

She was furious.

Nemesio and Hellen ran in after her.

Alessandria looked at Harrison.

"Call Court. Call our allies. Call the Nobility! We need to act!" she shouted.

We all rushed over to her.

Alessandria walked over to Harrison.

I instinctively grabbed her.

My dulled blade span faster.

She pulled me in for a hug. I tensed.

"What's going on, Alessandria?" Harrison asked.

Alessandria pressed her forehead against mine.

"Daniel. Mother. Is. dead," she said.

I remembered that that makes people sad so I hugged her and gently rubbed her back.

Alessandria gave a short laugh. "That doesn't affect you, does it?"

Now I needed to be tactful. As much as autism is a gift, it's a curse in these situations.

"No, no, no. That's terrible. Who else... Yes sorry I cannot fake this level of emotion," I said.

Alessandria playfully whacked me around the head.

Harrison still rolled himself over and kissed my hand. Well, if my Mother's death can get me sympathy. I'm not above using that for special stuff.

"What did you say about call our allies?" Harrison asked.

Alessandria looked me dead in the eye. "Mother is dead. The matriarch of our House is dead. I'll be crowd matriarch tomorrow night. I can't be-"

Nemesio hugged her. "Calm down. We need to think,"

Alessandria nodded and I didn't disagree. If we call Court now without the Order of the Divine Air's support. This law change would fail and we won't get another chance.

Hellen tapped her massive stick against her hands.

I turned to Harrison and felt back I was looking down on him. So, I knelt down to his level.

"If we get the Inquisitorial Order's support, will

you call Court as Regent?"

He didn't answer. Alessandria stepped forward. I pointed my finger at her like a warning.

"As Regent I have all the powers the Queen has in theory. I can call Court for the law change but you need to get the Order of the Divine Air to pledge to you. If not, I won't call Court,"

I nodded at Harrison. Then turned to Alessandria.

"How do we get the last Order to pledge themselves to us?" I asked.

Alessandria shook her head. "I don't know. We have so much to do. We need to get the Order to pledge themselves. Find the Word Bearer and kill him. Then we need to kill Fateweaver,"

I frowned at Fateweaver's name, that horrid man who could bend Fate to his Will and the man who murdered our Father.

Attempting to be a good brother, I said:

"Let's focus on one problem at a time-"

"Don't forget the mob attacks," Harrison said.

Nemesio frowned. "Harrison, what's going on with them?"

Hellen walked over.

"After my adventure the other week, the Church is massing a people's army. These mobs running riot. Attacking the innocent. Killing people and the like,"

We all listened. This was disgraceful. The Church was meant to be a peaceful organisation. I don't see how they are.

"The Procurators are stretched too thin. The military is helping but there are too many mobs," Harrison said.

"What about killing ya Church?" Hellen asked.

Me and Harrison would love that but that wasn't diplomatic apparently.

Alessandria smiled and ignored her. "Isn't the Church going to try and kill the Queen?"

Harrison nodded.

"Me and Harrison will focus on protecting the Queen. You three focus on getting the Order of the Divine Air pledged," I said.

Alessandria nodded and hugged me again.

"Are you okay? After this I promise we'll grief," she said in my ear.

I nodded and kissed her cheek.

Watching her, Hellen and Nemesio walk away, I think it was starting to hit me. My Mother was dead. My wonderful scheming clever Mother was dead.

14

CHAPTER 3

Listening to the roars of the crowd outside, Alessandria looked away from the stone window and pressed her back against the cold hard grey stone walls. The walls felt rough against her black leather armour.

Wanting to do something whilst she waited for Nemesio to come back with her drink, Alessandria looked around her bed chamber. Sadly her maid was far too good at her job.

The shiny red silk sheets were perfectly pressed and straight and tucked under the heavy mattress. With the maid dusting the large wooden bed posts and the crazy dragon headpieces were cleaned to perfection.

Even the smell of chemicals with a hint of peanuts was oddly pleasant and now Alessandria really craved nuts.

A part of Alessandria wanted to give the maid an extra tip. After all her and Nemesio had left the bed in a state last night. She smiled at the memory.

Looking away from the bed, Alessandria realised the maid had wiped down the cold stone floor and picked up her dress. Putting it back up perfectly. Maybe she'll have to train Nemesio to be this good. Or get the maid to work for Alessandria in the future.

Turning her attention, to the rough walls where paintings and relics hung. She didn't care about them. Alessandria dismissed them all as she thought about what happened.

Her Mother Kinaaz was dead. Definitely a loss for the entire country. One less scheming, cunning and unique woman in Ordericous. Granted Alessandria hadn't seen her Mother for two months as Kinaaz had been hunting down information on Fateweaver. But the thought of her Mother dying… that wasn't possible.

But it was.

It was very possible and it had happened. Her loving, scheming Mother was dead.

A part of Alessandria had wanted to go down to the crypt to see her body. But she didn't have the strength yet.

Hearing Nemesio come in, Alessandria smiled as she took the large wooden cup of deep dark black coffee. The cup warming her hands and the smell comforted her.

If this was a normal day, Alessandria knew she would smile as her strong beautiful Nemesio walked towards her in his red and blue fiery armour that highlighted his perfect body. But this wasn't a normal day.

Nemesio joined her in pressing his back against the wall as he drank his bright (almost luminescent) green tea.

"Are you okay?" Nemesio asked.

It was only then that Alessandria stood why

Daniel hated that question. It was such a stupid question. Her Mother had just died. Of course she wasn't okay!

Deciding to be the good girlfriend, Alessandria smiled.

"I don't know what I'm feeling. I feel angry, sad. I don't know,"

She wanted to ask about how he dealt with his mother being murdered by a Noble House when he was a young boy. But that seemed a little tactless.

"I am here for you if you want to talk. I... I know how it feels,"

Alessandria nodded,

A part of her mind wondered what her Mother would say to her now. When her Father died Kinaaz was devastated but she made sure Alessandria and Justin were okay. Then Alessandria remembered how her Mother had abandoned Daniel to his grief alone.

As much as she loved her Mother, Alessandria didn't think she could forgive Kinaaz for abandoning Daniel until this year.

"I need a distraction. What do you know about the Order of the Divine Air?" Alessandria asked.

Nemesio took a long slip of his tea.

"Well, they're very unique,"

"I'm sorry? The Order of the Blessed Earth- they were unique with their beliefs about nature. Your former Order- they were unique. They were extremists,"

Nemesio nodded. "Oh don't get me wrong. I

agree. In the Inquisition, we always stayed away from the Divine Air,"

"Why?"

"Their central tenant is only the air is holy and to be Holy you must be one with the air,"

Alessandria shook her head, not understanding. It sounded like the rubbish from the other Orders.

"Their current leader believes in burning people alive to make them Holy,"

Alessandria nodded and drank a mouthful of her coffee. Her mouth exploding with the rich fruity notes of the drink.

"Interesting. How do we get them to pledge?"

Nemesio shook his head. "I don't know. We'll meet with them and see how it goes. I think my Former Sage met with the leader once. Meeting went badly until the Sacred offered up a servant to be burnt,"

Alessandria really didn't want to meet the Sage of the Order of the Divine Air.

Nemesio turned onto his side to face her.

"Alessandria, we need to prepare for-"

Alessandria shot up. Walking away from Nemesio.

"No! I am not being crowned Matriarch. Daniel will be Head of our House,"

Nemesio opened his mouth.

"No. I am not ruling a Noble House. I am a Dominicus Procurator. I investigate crime. I don't rule,"

Nemesio closed his mouth.

"Daniel will be amazing. He needs to rule the House of Fireheart. Not me,"

"What if we fail? What if the law doesn't change?"

"I don't care. I'll run away. I'll leave Ordericous. Daniel must be made Lord Fireheart!"

"You would leave me?"

Alessandria stopped and looked at Nemesio. His beautiful eyes were so wide and fearful. His face was pale.

She slowly walked back over to him and pressed her back against the rough stone wall.

"Of course not. I love you Nemesio. I- I just can't be the Head of my Noble House. I don't want it. If that happens then my life of happiness is over,"

Nemesio nodded and kissed her.

"I won't let that happen. I need to check my records for something useful about the Divine Air. I'll be back," Nemesio said, giving Alessandria another kiss.

When the door slammed shut, Alessandria downed her amazing coffee and placed the wooden cup on the windowsill.

She crawled down to the floor. Her back against the rough stone wall and raised her knees to her face.

CHAPTER 4

Looking down at all the commoners below, I had to shake my head at them. This was ridiculous. Plain and simple.

All these people in all shapes and sizes screamed and shouting hate speech at the castle. They were packed so tightly together I couldn't see the grey cobblestone road below them.

Across the road or river of angry mobsters, I frowned as I saw fearful shop owners and children at the windows. Probably hoping the mob wouldn't attack or break the shops.

Feeling the solid rough yellow stone wall beneath my feet, I knew the castle would easily hold if there was an attack. But this was all pointless.

I remember a time when I stood on this wall with my Father looking out over the city. He made me promise to protect this place, and I fully intend to keep it.

Either side of me strong armoured men and women stood ready to unleash a hail of arrows and bullets at the mob. Some might say that was extreme.

For these were only brainwashed thuds of the Church.

Personally, I would have attacked already. No one should get this close to the castle. Even if the Procurators and the military are spread too thin.

My dulled blade spun in my hand as I attempted to think what to do next. Of course I had no power here. These weren't Fireheart troops and I was only the Military Broker to the Castle. But the men and women kept looking at me. I suppose getting married to the Lord Regent does have benefits.

Turning my attention back to the mob below, their sweat and dirt filled my nose. That was disgusting! These people needed to bathe not be here hammering down the Castle.

Speaking of which the violent sound of something smashing into the Castle's reinforced gates drew my attention. We needed to act that was true.

In this situation, I would just order the troops to open fire. Target the edges and work their way inwards. Giving no one the chance to escape and slaughtering all these mobsters. Sadly, I don't think the Queen would like that idea.

Thankfully, the sound of a massive wooden stick tapping against the stone floor made me smile.

Turning around, I had never been so happy to see Hellen in her grey Procurator cloaked with Alessandria and Nemesio walk up behind her.

Nemesio and Alessandria sneered at the mob below.

Hellen gave the mob a massive smile and tapped her massive stick in her hand.

Of course, she would be loving this. She always wants a good fight.

"This is unexpected," Alessandria said.

Trust her to be diplomatic.

"What should we do? I'm sure they'll listen to you," Nemesio said to Alessandria.

I was attempted to add Nemesio should capture them all and torture them like he did me. But that seemed a little uncalled for.

The screaming and shouting of the mob got louder. I turned to see the mob pointing and trying to throw things at me.

Hellen stepped forward.

"Calm the fuck down!"

We all looked at Hellen.

The mob stopped.

Alessandria quickly stepped forward.

"Everyone stop this. Please. Leave now and nothing bad will happen. Do you really want to be attacking the Queen? She is amazing and has done so much for all of us,"

The mob started laughing.

"That Queenie killed her Father! She was great. But she's corrupted," a man shouted from the mob.

A wave of agreeing shouts came from the mob.

"She's corrupted with the gay virus. We must kill her. She'll infect us all!" someone else said.

I stepped out of the view from the mob and busted out laughing. This was utter nonsense. The Queen would never have killed her father, and really? The gay virus?

When I become Lord Fireheart, it will definitely

do more to make higher education free for people. We wouldn't have all these stupid conspiracy theories if more people became educated.

A loud snap came from the Castle's gate.

Alessandria shouted orders.

The troops fired.

There were hundreds of mobsters down there.

Too many would escape.

I couldn't let that happen.

I looked around.

There was a rope nearby.

I grabbed it.

Tying it to the wall.

I climbed down.

Whipping out my sword.

The cobblestone was rough and chipped.

The mob saw me.

They screamed in delight.

They charged.

My sword slashed and lashed at them.

My sword sliced through arms, chests and necks.

Corpses dropped rapidly.

More foes came.

They dived for me.

I dodged them.

Thrusting my sword into their backs.

Fists slammed into my back.

I fell forward.

More people jumped down.

Hellen whacked them with her stick.

Bones shattered.

Skulls crushed.

I slashed and lashed through the mob.

People screamed.

People attacked.

Everyone died.

My sword bit into their bodies.

The warm blood sprayed up my body.

My face covered in blood.

Nemesio charged past.

Snapping necks.

Breaking backs.

Alessandria rushed past.

She swirled and twirled her blade.

Her sword slicing into victims.

Someone grabbed me.

I span.

Thrusting my blade into his stomach.

More mobsters charged.

I charged too.

I dived into the crowd.

Swinging, slashing and slicing my way through.

Arms were severed.

Heads were cracked.

Blood flooded the ground.

Someone tackled me.

Blade flashed past.

I raised my arm.

I grabbed a man's arm.

A blade got closer to my throat.

I lashed the man with my nails.

He screamed.

I whacked him in the face.

He fell off.

I split his throat.

More foes were coming.

I span.

Forty people were charging at me.

No allies were around.

A storm of arrows slaughtered them.

Forty corpses slammed to the ground.

Looking around, I saw hundreds of corpses lying there. Most of them with massive sharp arrows in them.

The cobblestone ground was turned dark red from all the blood. Even now, litres of blood poured from the corpses.

The sound of Hellen smashing skulls with her massive stick made me smile. Of course, someone needed to check they were all dead but Hellen definitely got too much pleasure from checking.

Hearing the sound of swelling breathing close by, I saw a half dead teenager crawling over to me. A blade in hand.

This boy had arrows deep in his back. He wasn't much younger than me. Maybe 18 or 19. I shook my head. This teenager shouldn't be here fighting. He should be living.

As he crawled closer, I stood on his hand with the blade. He swore under his breath.

"You're a disgrace!" the boy said. "You're an insult to men. You aren't even one,"

The boy spat at me.

I honestly felt sorry for the teenager. I pressed the point of my sword into his back.

"The Word Bearer was right," he said.

I lessened the pressure on my sword point.

"The Word Bearer said you were awful. I can smell how gay you are,"

"Who is the Word Bearer?"

"For the Triad!" the boy shouted. Pushing his back into my sword.

CHAPTER 5

Breathing in the last of the sweet flowery air before autumn really descended, Alessandria admired the rows upon the rows of stunning flowers as nature took its course.

Even now as the autumn started to kill the flowers, Alessandria loved it here. The cold sweet air chilling her skin and making her breath condense ever so slightly.

The sound of rustling leaves and beaches filled the air.

But there was something impressive about autumn too. Whilst the cold air killed off the once amazing flowers, there were a handful in each tens of metres long rows that stood firm and defiant. They weren't going to die just yet. They were going to brave the storm and survive the autumn.

A part of Alessandria could easily relate to that. The Church, the Triad and all the other threats banging on her preverbal door. They all wanted her dead. But Alessandria knew she needed to survive a little longer.

Turning her attention away from the dying rows of flowers, Alessandria turned to see the immense green ivy covered castle with Nemesio and Daniel standing there. Looking around for the Queen. Daniel's dulled blade spinning slowly.

As much as Alessandria wished Hellen was here that damn Queen's Dominicus Procurator ordered Hellen away from Alessandria. Hopefully, she could get Hellen back. Alessandria wanted her friend with her. That massive stick was handy.

A gust of freezing cold wind made Alessandria shiver. This was not a good place for a meeting with the Queen. Why couldn't the Queen meet them indoors? In the warmth?

Then Alessandria realised outside was probably the safest place to be. She knew for a fact the Church (and by extension the Triad) had agents and spies within the castle so outside away from them was probably a good idea.

In all honesty, Alessandria hated all of this. She felt like a noose was tightening around her neck. All she wanted was for her friends and family to be free to live in a country without evil masterminds and zealots wanting to kill them. Alessandria needed to see that happen even if it cost her her life.

The hint of amazingly sweet perfume in the cold wind made Alessandria look up and smile as she saw the Queen in her stunning pure white fur cloak walk towards them.

Walking over to Nemesio, Daniel and the Queen, Alessandria's feet twisted and turned in the soft muddy ground. Of course, the Queen was walking perfectly through it like some kind of angel.

"Lady and Master Fireheart pleasure to see you

both. Please accept my condolences about your Mother. She was an interesting but great Noblewomen," the Queen said.

Alessandria nodded her thanks and wondered what the Queen really wanted to say about her Mother. Sadly this was hardly the time though.

"Lady Alessandria, what do you have to report?" the Queen asked.

Alessandria paused for a moment, what did she have to report? That there was a massive mob raised by the Church and that was it.

Nemesio stepped forward. "The Church you know they're up to something. If you didn't you would have met us inside,"

Alessandria cocked her head. She knew she should have got that.

"Nemesio, my apologies. The situation has been dire for a while. All outer villages have been claimed by the Church and the Triad. Our military is stretched thin trying to reclaim the land,"

Daniel frowned. "Harrison. Is that why he's been away a lot?"

"Yes Master Fireheart. Do not be mad at him. It was me who encouraged him to keep it a secret,"

Daniel's eyebrows rose and Alessandria gave a small smile as she realised Daniel probably didn't know why he would be mad at Harrison being busy, and coming home later at night.

"The Triad has claimed the outer villages. What about the main City where we are?" Alessandria asked.

"We hold it by a thread. The Triad are coming for me. What do you know about the Word Bearer?"

"Your Majesty…" Alessandria didn't know what to say.

"Declare the Church Traitorous," Daniel said. Probably in a more demanding tone than he realised.

The Queen smiled. Her eyes narrowing on Daniel.

"A Queen does not simply declare the Dissolution of the Church. I want to. Their control of the people, the country and their brainwashing has annoyed me for a while. But-"

"The fate of the country rests on you. Forget politics," Daniel said.

As much as Alessandria agreed with Daniel, she walked over to the Queen.

"The Word Bearer is inside the Church,"

The Queen's face lit up.

"Nemesio, the Order of the Divine Air, didn't they try to dissolute the Church in their history?"

"Of course! They mapped each and every player in the Church. If anyone knows who the Word Bearer could be. It's them,"

"Lady, Master Fireheart take care. Nemesio protect them," the Queen said. She turned to Daniel. "Stay alive Master Fireheart, I have a wedding to perform,"

Daniel smiled and nodded.

As the Queen started to walk away, Alessandria

shouted: "I need Hellen back!"

"Already Commanded it,"

Alessandria smiled. At last there was a chance she would save Ordericous and hopefully she might get the Divine Air to pledge themselves to her. Alessandria might be able to save herself from her Fate after all.

CHAPTER 6

I was hardly impressed with... whatever this was. The meeting chamber inside the Order of The Divine Air's Headquarters was horrific. My dulled blade spun slowly as I looked at this ugly room.

All the walls of this large box room were covered in feathers. Some were very nice actually. All the feathers in a wonderful pattern of bright reds, blues, greens and some rather nice pinks too. It was strange though. Who decorates a room in feathers?

Even the floor was strange. It wasn't covered in feathers but Ash. The entire floor was covered in a thick layer of grey rough Ash. Making the air smelt faintly of charred bodies and freshly cooked chicken. A hint of juicy roasted chicken formed on my tongue.

At least the table in the middle of the room was normal. Well at first glance at least. The small round coffee table looked to be made from hard dark brown oak. Then I realised it was made from oak covered in the dried blood. I really didn't want to know who's blood that was.

The sound of birds shrieking and 'singing' could be heard in the distance so I guessed they had a bird enclosure nearby. From what I remember about the Divine Air they were mostly bird trainers by trade before they got into the Inquisition.

Wanting to look at something else besides these rainbow covered walls and massive wooden door, I turned to look at Alessandria in her black leather armour and Nemesio in that blue and red fiery armour.

Personally, I don't really know why Nemesio still wears it. He hasn't been an Inquisitor for months since we destroyed his order.

Then I remembered Alessandria mentioning it had something to do with Nemesio wanting to remember what he never wanted to be like again.

I completely agree. He was awful when I first met him. Hell, he got me tortured. My old scars pulsed pain up my arms as I thought about them.

Somehow thinking about my time in the torture chambers made me think of Mother. She was really gone. She was never going to scheme again or plot another successful thing. My beautiful Mother was gone and I hadn't even seen the body yet.

The sound of claws hopping along the floor made me look around. There wasn't a bird in here a moment ago. Then I looked at the table and there was an impressive orange phoenix hopping about on there.

That was weird.

The wooden door opened as a very strange man walked through. At least I think it was a man. Instead of a face, he had a large bird skull over his head. It was so big I couldn't see his real features.

Even his clothes, that presumably covered a slim but muscular body, were made from a rainbow of feathers. There were tens of shades and colours there. Everything from pink to deep blue to bright vibrant red. This was going to be interesting.

Looking at Alessandria, I saw she was equally confused if not more so. She stepped forward.

The man put up his arm and the phoenix flew over. Its sharp claws digging into his arm.

"Sage of Order of the Divine Air?" Alessandria asked.

The Sage nodded as he stroked his phoenix.

A part of me was actually interested in the bird. They were the creatures of myths and legends but to see one in real life was impressive.

"You are the Former Scared Fire?" the Sage asked.

"I am my Lord Sage. I don't think we ever got the opportunity to meet," Nemesio said.

"I made sure of that. Your Former Order was not my favourite. I am glad it is no longer," the Sage said.

I could hardly disagree but I hoped someone was going to get to the point. I would like to spend some time with beautiful Harrison today.

"You know the players in the Church, correct?" Alessandria asked.

"Of course, my Mentor and Former Sage of our Order wanted the Church destroyed once. I shall continue the work. The Church shall face the Air's judgement,"

Opening my mouth, I wanted to make a

comment, but Alessandria looked at me. I closed it.

"We're tracking a person called the Word Bearer-" Nemesio said.

The Sage stepped forward. His phoenix flew off his arm and circled us.

"The Word Bearer is powerful. He corrupts the Divine Air. He must be released so the Air Gods can judge him,"

This was getting strange.

"We agree, my Lord Sage. Who is the Word Bearer?" Nemesio asked.

The Sage went silent.

I looked around for the phoenix to see, it had disappeared.

"Sage, we also need your help. If I promise to dissolve the Church when I'm in power. Will you pledge us your support?" I asked.

Alessandria looked as if she was going to moan at me for being so forward. But she stopped and turned to the Sage. His bird skulled face looked down to the floor.

"The Air and the Air Gods want to. But we can't. The Air must focus on the Word Bearer. Kill him and we have a deal. If not, we will never pledge to you,"

Nemesio stepped forward.

The phoenix appeared.

"We need your help! Help us! Tell us who the Word bearer is!" Nemesio shouted.

"No. The Gods want me to help you then you must kill the Word Bearer. It is the Will of the Gods,"

I wanted to surge forward. Thrusting my blade into his chest. What would the Gods Will then? But I spun my dulled blade faster.

The phoenix and Sage left.

Walking over to Alessandria and Nemesio, I felt the soft, thick ash move under my feet. It felt awful.

Alessandria got us in a circle. "This is stupid. Nemesio, did you give that Inquisitor outside the offering?"

Nemesio nodded.

"The Inquisition is stupid. They want us to kill the Word Bearer. But we need their help to do that. stupid!" I said.

Alessandria shook her head.

"We're going to have to find the Word Bearer ourselves. We know he's something in the Church. We'll start there," Alessandria said.

For some strange reason, I placed my hand gently on Alessandria's shoulder.

"Nemesio, can you do some research please? I need Alessandria,"

Nemesio nodded and Alessandria came close to my ear.

"What's wrong?"

"I need to see Mother,"

CHAPTER 7

The smell of damp and fatty candles that made the taste of bacon form on her tongue was the smell of the crypt. Alessandria took a deep breath before stepping any closer.

In all honesty, she was glad Daniel had made her come to see Mother. Otherwise Alessandria might never have come. Just the thought of seeing her Mother's body made Alessandria's stomach churn.

Forcing herself to look ahead, Alessandria focused on the dark grey stone blocks that formed this little section of the crypt. She could feel the cold coming from them and everything was gently chilled down here.

Considering this was a crypt in the castle, Alessandria would have imagined this viewing room would be more ornate. But at least the crypt had a beautiful domed ceiling with little flecks of gold and scripture embedded in the stone.

She remembered her Father making a joke about the scripture here after his Mother died. He said it was a waste of paper. You need magic to protect the soul, not paper.

The thought of her family being lesser magic users gave Alessandria some comfort about her Mother's soul. Even though she wasn't sure she believed in such things.

Making herself look at the coffin itself that sat on an impressively plain black stone altar. Alessandria admired the level of skill involved in the coffin. As she looked at the little details and flicks of the painting as someone had decided to paint a timeline of her Mother's life on the coffin. Alessandria didn't know if it was nice or pointless.

Seeing Daniel arched over the coffin, his black leather trench coat and trousers making him almost blend into the crypt, Alessandria took a deep breath and walked over to the coffin.

Slowly looking at her Mother's body, Alessandria frowned as she had to look at her tall, slim Mother with her well aged features dressed in her long silky white wedding dress. This wasn't pleasant.

Alessandria thought about the times she had held her Mother's hands, now cold and lifeless, and spoke to her. But now her Mother's lips were thin, dry and cracked.

A part of her wanted her strong beautiful Nemesio with her but she knew this was a family matter. Her and Daniel needed to do this alone.

"She was special, wasn't she?" Daniel said.

Alessandria wasn't sure if that was emotion she detected in his voice.

"Definitely. She really did everything for us,"

"For you more than me,"

Alessandria didn't know how to respond to that.

"She did love you, Daniel. Sure she didn't even

try to understand you until recently but she loved you,"

Daniel looked away from the coffin.

"I know she did. She really tried recently. I just wish she tried after I tried to kill myself,"

"I thought it was Mother who got the doctors and witch to you,"

Daniel nodded at that comment.

"And she was being abused by Justin,"

"To protect you. You were off limits. I clearly wasn't. Or maybe Mother thought Justin destroying my life was enough damage,"

Alessandria walked over to Daniel and hugged him. Surprisingly enough, Daniel buried his face into her shoulder. Daniel's nose was annoyingly pointy.

"We are a strange lot, aren't we? Mother a schemer. Father died a war hero. A gay son who tried to kill himself and a Daughter who's perfect," Daniel said.

Alessandria wasn't sure how to take the last bit.

"Daniel, I'm not perfect. I love you but I do get jealous sometimes,"

Daniel looked up at her. "I know you aren't perfect. But why are you jealous of me? I'm a no body, a freak, a family embarrassment,"

Alessandria gave an accidental laugh.

"That's rubbish, Daniel. A No One. Seriously? You've helped save the kingdom tens of times. A freak to people who don't care or even try to understand you. A family embarrassment. Really?

There's no one I'm prouder of. I'm proud to call you my brother,"

Daniel smiled.

Alessandria gave him a kiss on the head and she wandered over to her Mother's body.

Looking at her Mother's cold pale lifeless hands, they were laying in fists which was odd considering she never formed a fist in her life- on purpose.

"Daniel, what did Mother die of?"

"The doctors said Heart Attack, but they noted rigour lasted a lot longer than normal. They had to dress her whilst her body was in rigour,"

Alessandria nodded. Touching her Mother's hand, she felt a sharp pulse of cold travel up her arm. Alessandria really didn't want to do this.

Carefully, Alessandria uncurled her Mother's hands and something fell out. Landing on the soft cushioned fabric of the coffin.

Picking it up Alessandria realised it was a piece of rough musty old parchment. Daniel walked over to her.

Opening it Alessandria frowned as she saw lots of ancient scripture from various religions. But there was a passage circled in thick black ink.

Alessandria read it: "He lives in between all the lives of us and he rests in front of the Loom of Fates. Falling asleep as he weaves the Loom,"

Both siblings looked at each other wide eyed.

"That's what The Flamesword said to us about Fateweaver," Alessandria said.

"Mother found something and she died for it,"

"I thought Father made sure Fateweaver couldn't influence our family,"

"No, Alessandria. Only directly. Someone else could have been influenced to kill Mother,"

Alessandria nodded.

Turning her attention back to the parchment, there was another line or two that made been highlighted.

"The Loom of Our Fate and Faith are the Same. In the House of the Gods, the Fates are Weaved for all to die," Alessandria said.

Daniel took a few steps back. "Mother gave us everything we need. The Loom has to be in the Grande Cathedral, the head of the Church,"

"Of course but something still feels off. If the Fates have been weaved by it's fated for the Queen to be attacked,"

Daniel frowned. "I'll stay here to protect the Queen and Harrison. You, Nemesio and Hellen go to the Grande Cathedral. Hellen should have returned by now,"

Alessandria slowly nodded. She knew this was a sound plan but something told her she didn't want to leave her brother. It was too dangerous. She just lost her Mother. Alessandria couldn't face losing Daniel. But it was her Duty to find Fateweaver and she might find out more about the Word Bearer on the way.

Alessandria gave Daniel a massive hug. "Stay safe, Daniel. I love you. Just stay safe please,"

Daniel kissed her on the cheek. "Come back to me, Alessandria. I need my Maid of Honour,"

CHAPTER 8

When I had said to Alessandria I would protect the Queen I didn't think I would be faced with thousands of mobsters at my feet. But that's life I suppose?

As I looked down from the high grey stone castle walls, I saw thousands of angry mobsters staring back at me. All of them were people from different classes, areas of Ordericous and jobs. Yet they were all here to moan at the Queen.

Well, I say moan but judging by the looks I was getting these people wanted to kill.

Again I felt sorry for the people in the shops across the Castle. Men, women and children were at the windows their eyes widened. They probably barracked their shops just in case.

A drop of sweat ran down my spine as the warm midday sun beat down upon us.

A part of me wanted to find some essential oils to put under my nose because these people stunk. The air was thick with disgusting sweat and other foul odours.

The sound of their shouting the same stupid religious nonsense over and over was starting to annoy me. I mean yes keep shouting stuff but change it up!

If I hear one more passage from Saint Arthur the Third I'm going to kill these people. Well, I'll probably do that anyway.

Seeing the Queen step forward to my left, I had to admire her. She knew she was going to lose this argument but, with her stunning angelic white battle armour, at least she could lose in style.

Thankfully there were six guards forming a box like defence around us in case someone attacked the Queen. It still didn't make me feel any easier.

My dulled blade spun quicker as I looked at Harrison on my right. I really didn't want him here. This was dangerous. I couldn't let anything happen to him.

Just admiring his beautiful longish blond hair and his perfect face as he sat in his wheelchair, I knew I might need to make an impossible choice later on. The Queen or the love of my life.

Making a little cough, my attention returned to the Queen as I saw her stepping forward. My body tensed. My hand on the cold hilt of my sword.

"Mighty Citizens of Ordericous," the Queen said.

A wave of screaming and throwing fruit followed. Thankfully none of the fruit made it anywhere near the top of the wall.

"I understand you are angry but you have all been lied to. The Church is feeding you lies. I did not kill my Father and there is no such thing as the gay virus,"

I have to give it to her. She was trying. Failing but trying.

"Please stop this. I am not your enemy. I have transformed this country for the betterment of you. I serve all of you,"

Hundreds of fists banged on the Castle's gate.

The mob turned furious.

"Please calm down. I am telling you the truth. I am not the enemy. The Church is deceiving you,"

The Guards around us looked at each other.

Harrison rolled forward a little bit.

"As Queen I only want the best for you but do not become the puppet of others. Do not do the Church's dirty work for them,"

People screamed.

Flames engulfed a shop across us.

The Guards looked at each other nodding.

Harrison went to roll forward. I grabbed his wheel.

Something was wrong.

The mob banged on the Castle gate.

Magical energy crackled in the air.

The guards whipped out their swords.

They swung at the Queen.

I tackled her to the ground.

I jumped up. My sword hungry.

Slashing the throat of one guard.

The Queen leapt up.

Whipping out her swords.

They glowed bright red and blue.

The Queen attacked.

Her swords lashing through armour and bone.

I looked for Harrison.

He snapped the neck of a Guard.

Something was wrong.

He snapped the neck of a new Guard.

There were more traitors.

We had to move.

A Guard slammed his fists into me.

I fell forward.

Almost falling over the wall.

I spun around.

A guard charged at me.

I dodged him.

Kicking him as he charged.

Throwing him off the wall.

His body cracked on impact.

The mob's banging got louder.

Something cracked.

The Queen roared.

Her swords swirling, twirling and slashing at the enemy.

More Guards charged at her.

I surged forward.

Thrusting my sword into chests and backs.

Blood poured from the wounds.

I carved a bloody path to the Queen.

Guards screamed as I kicked them.

Shattering bones into deadly shards.

We needed to move.

The Queen waved at me.

She pointed to somewhere.

I looked.

She pointed to a little-

I ducked.

A Guard's sword swung past.

Harrison charged forward.

His chair knocking the foe.

Giving me time to snap his neck.

I threw the corpse off the wall.

I looked up.

The Queen pointed to a little wooden shed.

I nodded.

The Queen slaughtered a group of enemy guards.

So many traitors!

The Castle gates exploded.

It shook the entire wall.

Harrison rolled forward.

I grabbed him.

Thousands of voices screamed in delight.

The mob was inside the castle.

We needed to move!

The Queen sliced and diced the enemy.

I protected our rear.

Harrison pushed on.

The Queen's sword crackled with magical energy.

A burst of power exploded.

The enemy froze.

I didn't care what happened.

I ran over to Harrison.

Pushing him forward.

We were off the wall now.

The soft cobblestone ground felt strange as I ran.

Harrison gripped his chair.

I couldn't blame him.

The wooden shed was only a few metres away.

The mob screamed again.

They charged.

The Queen opened the shed's door.

I felt the enemy getting closer.

I charged into the shed.

The Queen followed.

She muttered something and the shed started humming. I thought I heard the mob banging on the wooden shed, but it sounded so faint and distant.

Looking around I was a bit confused why we were in here. There was nothing except a large wooden chest in the centre of the little shed.

The Queen kicked it and it opened. Revealing a staircase deep under the castle.

The Queen looked at Harrison. Her eyes fearful and surprisingly motherly.

"Leave me," Harrison said, quietly.

I ignored him and picked him up. The Queen carried his wheelchair. (Thank God it was light) No one was being left behind today!

CHAPTER 9

Hiding behind the edge of a massive stone tower in the Castle's wall, Alessandria hated the feel of the rough grey stone that chilled her fingers as she carefully looked over to the mob.

All Alessandria could see were the mobsters shouting and screaming. Presumably at the Queen. She remembered Daniel had said the Queen wanted to give a speech to try and get the mobsters to stand down. Alessandria always admired her friend's commitment to being a good Queen but this was foolish.

Even from tens of metres away, Alessandria could smell the sweat and utterly foul body odour of the commoners in all their different clothes and sizes.

To a professor or someone, it was probably amazing The Church had United all these different people against the one person who actually cared about them. But Alessandria hated this manipulation. It was cowardly. If the Word Bearer wanted to attack, he should be attacking. Not hiding behind deception and pulling the mob's strings.

The screaming and shouting grew louder like a bad choir. The hard cobblestone ground under her feet broke as Alessandria turned her feet.

She really wanted to run over to the mob and fight them. If anything to protect the Queen and Daniel. She needed to fulfil her duty. Then Alessandria remembered in this case her duty was to go to the Grande Cathedral to find the Loom of Fate and hopefully Fateweaver. It didn't make Alessandria feel any easier.

A memory of her beautiful Mother popped into her head. Her Mother once said sometimes scheme's require an extra piece that you don't like but the scheme still needs it regardless. Maybe her Mother was right. Alessandria didn't want to leave but her scheme to find Fateweaver needed it.

The sound of a massive wooden stick tapping against stone reminded Alessandria she wasn't alone in her mission. As she turned around and looked at her stunning Nemesio in his strong blue and red fiery armour. And her amazing friend Hellen in her dirty grey Procurator cloak.

With these two she could do anything.

Alessandria was about to speak but the air started to crackle gently with magical energy and the sound of the mob got even louder.

Peeking around the edge of the tower again, Alessandria frowned as she saw the mob attacking.

Of course, Alessandria (and definitely Hellen) wanted to go off and fight but they had a mission to do.

"We need to go," Nemesio said.

Alessandria wanted to disagree. What if her brother got hurt? Could she really live with herself if that happened?

Feeling a massive wooden stick tap her ankles, Alessandria turned to see Hellen pointing away from the mob.

At first Alessandria just thought Hellen wanted to go but when she looked down the street of shops and houses. Alessandria was hardly impressed. Patrols of mobsters in small groups were walking around.

"This is an attack. I don't think they want any alive," Alessandria said.

"Ya but we gonna move,"

For once Alessandria was surprised Hellen didn't want to charge in and whack people. Yet her friend was still right.

"Come on," Alessandria said.

Both Nemesio and Hellen nodded. Their weapons in hand.

Looking around, Alessandria noted the long grey cobblestone road with side streets every few metres. Even the tall colourful shops and houses on either side of the street were perfect hiding spots.

Crouching Alessandria led Nemesio and Hellen through the street. The cobblestone made her feet cold as they move.

All three of them constantly checked their surroundings. Alessandria wasn't taking any chances.

Their first side street was coming up on the left. Alessandria raised her sword. It was clear.

She hoped they all would be.

Knowing Nemesio and Hellen were checking

around them, Alessandria focused ahead. The Grande Cathedral was at the bottom of this long street that basically ran the entire length of Ordericous' Capital.

The screaming and shouting of the mob were far in the distance now. That gave Alessandria little comfort.

She felt Hellen tapping her gently on her shoulder.

Alessandria turned around to see Hellen pointing to a side street they passed.

She whipped out her sword.

Hellen whacked Alessandria to the side.

Alessandria spun around.

Three men with knives charged.

Hellen had saved Alessandria from a surprise attack.

Alessandria charged forward.

She jumped into the air.

Kicking the men as she landed.

Two men went down.

Their skulls cracking on impact.

Blood flooded out from the skull.

Hellen whacked the last man.

His neck shattered.

The corpse fell with a thud.

Alessandria looked around.

Coast was clear.

They all broke into a run.

Alessandria's feet pounded into the cobblestone.

She heard more voices.

More foes were here.

More side streets were coming up.

Five men stormed out.

They fired crossbows.

Alessandria dived to one side.

The enemy reloaded.

Her and Hellen charged.

The men struggled to reload.

Alessandria didn't care.

She lashed their chests.

Pieces of ribs and flesh spattered up the wall.

Hellen smashed her stick into their faces.

The crossbows fell to the ground.

Their faces crumbled.

Nemesio grunted.

Alessandria spun.

He was duelling with two women.

Alessandria grabbed a crossbow.

She aimed.

She fired.

The bolts shot into the women's heads.

They needed to move.

Alessandria ran. Her friends behind her.

Screams and shrieks filled the street.

They weren't fearful.

They were happy.

Alessandria kept running. She looked behind her.

A massive mob saw them.

Alessandria's eyes widened.

They had to run!

She ran as fast as she could.

Hellen and Nemesio copied her.

Bottles flew through the air.

They smashed next to her.

Glass shards flying through the air.

The mob was gaining.

They couldn't fight this.

Alessandria saw something out of the corner of her eye.

It was a stick.

It was Hellen's stick.

Alessandria turned slightly.

Hellen was running away.

Her heart raced.

What was Hellen doing?

Nemesio ran away too.

Alessandria wanted to pause.

She wanted to stop.

She couldn't.

Why were they running?

A bottle flew straight past her.

Alessandria saw her friends running into some ruins.

More bottles smashed around her.

Alessandria followed her friends.

She hoped they could lose the mob in the ruins.

CHAPTER 10

I might not know who built the castle and this network of secret passages but I'll admit they were considerate builders.

Gently pushing Harrison in his wheelchair, the wooden handles of the chair feeling warm and rough in my hands. I had to appreciate these secret tunnels.

All around us the smooth oily black stone was perfectly chipped to make the tunnel a perfect circle. With a textured floor that gave the tunnel just enough grip so no one would slip but not too much to make someone have to walk carefully.

My dulled blade rested gently between my fingers as I continued to push Harrison.

Although, these builders clearly didn't build the tunnels to smell great. The smell of dead, stale air filled my nose. I really wanted some fresh air about now.

Ahead of us the Queen was like a beacon of bright white light as she walked with her now dirty white armour. Her two swords glowing with bright light blue magical energy that made the air hum slightly.

As I looked down at my beautiful Harrison, the Queen's magical light made his longish blond hair even more perfect and stunning. Harrison held a sword we had found earlier in the tunnels just in case.

I had to take a deep breath as I stupidly thought about Harrison having to defend himself. Could he?

Then I remembered a paralysed soldier I served with years ago and... wow, he could kill. I supposed that slightly eased my mind but I still wanted to will Harrison away to safety.

Hoping to think about something more positive, my mind thought about Alessandria. She had meant what she said in the crypt. We both needed each other to come back. We were the only ones we had left besides Harrison. I wasn't going to lose anyone else close to me.

The humming in the air grew louder and the Queen's bright lights were growing in intensity. At least the smell of stale air lessened.

"What's wrong?" I asked.

"Someone's coming. There's a danger, Master Fireheart," the Queen said.

Harrison raised his sword. Almost taking my eye out.

"Who?" I asked.

The Queen didn't answer.

I felt something icy wash over me. It was like little pieces of ice were growing over my skin. I checked Harrison nothing.

"Ice," I said.

The Queen didn't seem to understand what I was

talking about. But this all felt familiar like I had been through this before.

Then I remembered when Fateweaver Primus had taken over my Flesheater Ability, but I don't feel like I want to use it. And I had banished her from my mind last time.

The Queen looked at me. Her eyes interested but concerned. Stroking my face, I felt a thick layer of ice starting to harden on my skin.

Then I remembered. I had experienced this before. It was a brief encounter. I hadn't told anyone about it. But I had met Fateweaver before.

He attacked me when I was in Mortisical as a soldier. He froze me before he showed himself.

"Fateweaver," I said quietly.

"So this is where you hide from my mob. Interesting. I would be impressed. If not I had written this part in your Fate," a deep voice said.

Yet this voice was strange. I tried to listen closely to it, but it felt like the voice slipped away before I could focus on it.

"How are you Daniel Fireheart? Are you cold? Can you move?" the voice asked.

I went to step forward, but I couldn't.

The Queen walked over to me. She kicked me in the leg. I couldn't feel it.

"Fateweaver, your Mother is gone," I said.

A quiet snarl echoed around the tunnel.

"Your Mother was clever. Hiding a shard of her soul in the Flesheater gene. I still killed her. I still bested her. Your Mother was weak and pathetic,"

A deafening snarl echoed all around us.

It came from a thousand different directions.

I could move.

I grabbed Harrison's wheelchair.

We ran.

The Queen ran ahead.

A dark shadowy figure appeared.

The Queen slashed her sword at it.

Nothing happened.

The figure disappeared.

I felt something behind me.

I spun around.

A dark shadowy hand grabbed my throat.

Harrison rolled forward.

Thrusting his sword through the figure.

The figure snarled.

The hand squeezed.

Air rushed out of my lungs.

I was choking.

I was gagging.

My lungs screamed for air.

The Queen charged over.

Slamming her fists into the figure.

He let go.

The Figure coughed.

The Queen went to kick him.

The Figure disappeared.

She grabbed Harrison's chair.

We all ran through the tunnel.

"What was that?" Harrison asked.

"An ancient foe. A demon. I tried to control it. Fateweaver must have bonded to it," the Queen said.

"A demon!" I shouted.

"Your sister can explain. I've doomed us all,"

Harrison's chair exploded.

Harrison was thrown to the ground.

The shadowy demon reappeared.

Harrison raised his sword.

The demon slashed its claw.

Catching Harrison's sword.

The sword melted.

I jumped on the demon.

Smashing my fists into its face.

My legs wrapped around the demon.

Squeezing.

The demon snarled in pain.

It fell towards the wall.

I grabbed its head.

Smashing its demonic skull into the wall.

Again and again and again.

The demon snarled.

Its shadowy claws grabbed me.

Cutting into my shoulder.

I screamed.

The Queen muttered something in a dead language.

It shrieked.

My ears bleed.

The demon disappeared.

Without checking if the coast was clear, I picked up Harrison and carried him as I followed the Queen who was already walking away from us.

I didn't know what she had done but I could see... she was scared. Our brave, wonderful Queen was scared. And that scared the hell out of me. What wasn't she telling me?

CHAPTER 11

Her Father had once told Alessandria mobs were pretty stupid. At the time Alessandria had moaned saying that it was unfair to treat criminals as stupid. Even now she stood by that but when it came to mobs, her Father was probably right.

Laying down on a beam of ancient smooth black marble listening to the call of birds and crash of the waves hundreds of metres away, Alessandria stared down on the rest of the historical site.

But she was a little unsure about the marble she was laying on because whilst it was a thick marble beam. The massive marble pillars it rested on had definitely crumbled over the years.

Trying to ignore that fact, Alessandria looked out on the amazing historical site. For hundreds of metres around her large yellow and grey stone structures laid in ruin. Like an earthquake had destroyed a city. Leaving homes, churches and castles half standing.

The smell of the fresh salty sea air made Alessandria sneeze which tens of metres off the ground meant nothing. That wasn't going to attract the mob. But she did fancy some fish and chips as the taste of salt covered her tongue.

Looking back at the ruins below, Alessandria remembered reading something about this place in her *Procurator Times* magazine. Apparently some drug dealers had used the site as a lab. And apparently there was a secret chamber somewhere still filled with the toxic fumes.

Alessandria knew it would be cruel but if she could find that chamber. Her mob problems might go away.

Turning her head slightly, Alessandria saw a massive twisted oak tree with dark yellow leaves and as she looked at it. She thought she could smell something chemical nearby.

Alessandria smiled as she noticed something cracked on the bottom of the tree. From this height it was impossible to tell what it was. A door? A gap in the tree? But it was still a lead.

The sound of a stick whacking stone made Alessandria frown as she knew Hellen was warning the mob were entering the ruins. Alessandria just hoped Hellen would be safe.

A few moments later, Alessandria saw a massive mob of black and white tunics walk into the ruins. Running around searching the destroyed buildings for them. She needed a plan. She couldn't fight all of them.

The sound of something moving next to her made her turn to see her beautiful Nemesio crawling up next to her. His blue and red fiery armour dusty and covered in dirt.

"What now?" Alessandria asked.

Nemesio shrugged. "I don't know. This was

Hellen's plan,"

Alessandria knew Hellen was a loyal reader of the Procurator Times (mainly because the hot drawings of some of the criminals and the male Procurators) so Hellen must know about the lab with the toxins.

"I need to reach that oak over there but I need a distraction," Alessandria said.

Nemesio smiled. "Leave it to me,"

She gave Nemesio a quick kiss before Alessandria crawled along the marble beam towards the pillar closest to the oak.

As she moved, feeling the warm marble pressing against her body, Alessandria heard Nemesio's distraction.

"Mobsters!" Nemesio shouted.

Alessandria shook her head. She was almost at the pillar.

"Over here stupid!" Nemesio shouted again.

The mob started to shout and scream at him. At least their attention was on him and not Alessandria. But Alessandria knew she didn't have much time.

"You are all traitors!"

Alessandria cocked her head, not the most original of Nemesio's lines but the mob seemed to hate it.

Approaching the pillar, Alessandria could see it clearer now. The massive pillar was oily black with massive chunks taken out of it. Presumably because of it breaking over time.

Hopefully, she could use the broken chunks to

climb down but Alessandria was hardly the best climber.

"You are all silly little puppets. The Queen is innocent. You are all wrong!"

Alessandria tapped her head against the top of the pillar as she started to climb down it. Why Nemesio wanted to make the mob really mad was beyond her.

Climbing down, Alessandria's hand burned as the pillar released its heat from the sun. The rough texture and constantly having to look where to place her foot wasn't making this easier.

Alessandria heard voices.

She looked down.

Three mobsters were at the bottom of the pillar.

Someone shot out.

Whacking them with a stick.

Blood squirted out of the wounds.

They didn't even get a chance to scream.

Alessandria finished her climb and nodded her thanks to Hellen.

Walking over the massive oak, Alessandria knew the chemical smell would be stronger here and even the odd patch of grass looked diseased and dead.

Hellen walked ahead of Alessandria and pointed to the crack Alessandria had seen earlier. The large black gap in the oak tree looked like some kind of door.

Hellen tapped it.

Green gas came out.

Alessandria threw Hellen to the side. This was definitely the place.

"Alessandria Fireheart," a deep male voice said from behind her.

Turning around, Alessandria was surprised to see a little girl no older than 8 standing there. Her skin youthful and her clothes posh, expensive.

"I have no idea who this girl is but I thought you would hardly kill a child," the male voice continued.

Alessandria pointed her sword towards the child.

"Probably for the best Alessandria. I probably killed this child when I entered her mind,"

"Fateweaver?" Alessandria said quietly.

The child smiled wider than was naturally possible.

"Fateweaver. You have heard of me. That is excellent. Killing you will be even better," the child said.

Alessandria heard the mob getting closer.

"What do ya want?" Hellen asked.

"Darling Hellen, I want what we all want. Alessandria to die. The Firehearts to die. The Ordericousians to die!"

The mob started laughing.

Alessandria spun.

They were metres away.

The child walked towards Alessandria.

It whipped out a blade.

Alessandria couldn't kill it.

It was a child.

Hellen whacked the child with her stick.

It fell to the floor.

Hellen nodded.

Alessandria looked at the child. She knew such a young life would be killed as soon as Fateweaver entered its mind. But still.

Someone grabbed her wrist.

Alessandria tensed.

Raising her fist.

It was Nemesio.

The mob were advancing.

Alessandria and the others ran back.

The mob were about to walk past the oak.

Alessandria stopped.

She ran towards the oak.

Nemesio tried to grab her.

The mob charged forward.

Alessandria slashed and lashed her sword.

Chopping through flesh and bone.

She reached the oak.

She thrusted her sword into the gap.

Green gas poured out.

Alessandria held her breath.

She ripped out her sword.

The mob started coughing.

Alessandria fled.

When they were at least twenty metres from the mob, Alessandria stopped to see the mob coughing to death. They were all choking. Some were even vomiting black bile and their guts.

So many people died for nothing. Fateweaver would answer for this. That wasn't a threat. It was Fate.

CHAPTER 12

Whilst I had no idea where we were going in the slightest, I'll admit I was rather calm about it all.

Walking through the dark black stone tunnels with their smooth perfectly circular walls, I covered my nose with Harrison's smooth hand as I smelt something damp and mouldy. Probably a dead rat. Although, the weirdest thing happened because a hint of freshly roasted chicken formed on my taste buds. I guess everything does taste like chicken?

Surprisingly enough, my beautiful Harrison wasn't heavy to carry as I had him thrown over my shoulder. And I gently rubbed his legs as we walked. Of course I knew it was pointless because he couldn't feel it. But I knew I was trying to comfort him.

I wasn't sure if I was mad at myself yet for bringing him along, not that I had a choice or anything. I think when you truly love someone you just blame yourself for everything bad that happens to them. I just needed to keep him alive so I could marry him. After everything we've been through, I have to marry the love of my life.

Turning my dulled blade slowly, I looked ahead to see the Queen and her bright white glowing swords continuing to lead us on. Yet as I looked at her I saw utter fear in her eyes.

In fact, she had been afraid, no terrified since the demon attack. That horrid shadowy demon thing still concerned me. It had destroyed Harrison's wheelchair.

A part of me knew I had to ask the Queen about it. Especially as she said she had released it, but was this the right time?

The sound of the Queen's quiet footsteps got quieter as she started to stop.

I wanted to ask what was going on but I didn't get a chance before the Queen stopped and slowly opened the wall. Revealing a square stone door.

She only opened it slightly. A thin beam of light entering the tunnel. The Queen placed her finger over my mouth as she looked at me. Waving me forward.

The closer I got to the throne room the stronger the smell of sweet flowery perfume and Mur filled my senses.

Looking through the little opening of the door, I saw the golden murals and long sheets of bright pink silk on the walls of the throne room.

Harrison readjusted himself on me.

Turning my head, I managed to see the edge of something golden with rubies and other precious gems in it. I couldn't see all of it but I could make out it was the throne.

But someone was sitting on it. I couldn't see who.

Taking a step back, my mind spun a little. The Queen walked forward to look at the throne room. So this was clearly a coo of some sort. The Church persuaded the masses to turn against the beloved and righteous Queen. Allowing the Head of the Church what? To be King?

If that's true then how does the Word Bearer and Fateweaver fit in?

The Queen shot back. She raised her hands to her face.

I stepped forward and the Queen pointed to towards the small gap of light.

Stepping forward, my eyes widened and my Flesheater ability pulsed with blood lust as I looked at the source of all my pain. (Well all the gay pain anyway)

The man I was looking at was perfectly aged with smooth youthful features with a few wrinkles around the eyes. His long healthy limbs were impressively young for how old the man actually was. Even his long angelic white robes with gold highlights were perfectly intact. Showing no age. Considering the robes themselves were a few hundred years old.

Yet the real source of my anger was twofold. There was a strange crown like object on his head made from daggers and each one was coated in blood. Some gays would say the blood of my people.

Normally I refrain from too much association with wider gay culture but they would be right. It was the blood of my people. It was an outrageous tradition of the Head of the Church to hunt down nine gay people and kill them before they ascended to the House of Gods.

Each dagger was covered in a thick layer of dried blood. Each one must have killed tens of gays, and for what? Some title? Some pretty mansion and cathedral?

As much as I wanted to throw open this door and rip his throat out, I knew that wouldn't be wise. This dickhead was never alone.

But he would be. I would kill all his supporters and friends in the end. He would be alone. Just like me in the past because of his laws and stupid ideology.

Harrison started to slam his fists into my back.

"What?" I said, quietly.

He slapped my back even harder.

I turned around.

My eyes widened.

The shadowy humanoid demon stood there.

His long shadowy claws slicing up the air.

The Queen stopped.

She frowned.

The demon cocked its head and went to stroke Harrison's leg. I pointed a finger at it as a warning.

It looked like the demonic creature was laughing but no sound came out.

The demon waved us towards the door.

I don't know why but we all complied.

Harrison buried his face into my lower back as I stepped forward the stone door. The throne room was just like I imagined but it was deformed. Like Fateweaver or whatever power was in the castle had twisted the room into something... wrong.

I knew the throne room had long immensely beautiful golden walls with stunning depictions of our mighty past. From battles to weddings to treaty signings. Well except for the gold blank wall next to the throne.

But this all still felt wrong. Then I noticed the horrible smell of death and decay and the long black mouldy sheets of silks that hand off the walls.

It was like this entire place was corrupted or something.

There were hundreds of mobsters packed tightly into the throne room. They were always different shapes, classes and sizes but this time, they were wearing a black uniform. There was even a strange symbol over their chest but I couldn't make it out.

The demon pushed us through the crowd until we made it to the throne. The Queen gasped in horror. I couldn't blame her.

I remember the throne from paintings and this is not the Ordericousian Throne. The beautiful gold had turned flaky and black like a disease festering inside.

The once stunning precious gems that were embedded into the throne had fallen out. The throne was rotten and dying so the gems just fell out. It wasn't right. We needed answers.

The Queen stepped forward and spat at the Head of The Church.

"The Gods made a mistake making you Queen," he said, his voice righteousness and arrogant.

"The Gods did not Will you to do this. The Gods entrusted me to rule, not some puppet for their will," the Queen said.

This argument was going to be interesting.

"You do not know their Will. You are a woman. A weak woman. The Gods were mistaken to trust such an important task to your pathetic sex,"

So, he's a homophobe, sexist, what else?

"It is not your right to judge how I rule,"

"It is actually. The Gods made me Warden of the Faith of Ordericous. I protect the Faithful. You seek to destroy Faith,"

In all honesty, I would support her if she wanted that.

"You are not a Warden. You pretend to know what the Gods want but you know nothing. You don't even Bear their Words properly,"

What did she say?

My eyes widened as I realised what was happening.

"You're the Triad. You're the Word Bearer." I said, stepping forward.

The Word Bearer smiled and nodded.

"My plan has worked little gay. You are meaningless. You act so clever and you are still too late. Clearly gays aren't as clever as us real men,"

Seriously!

Harrison struggled. I held him firm.

"And look at your infirm boyfriend. Even that name is an assault on morality. Kill him," the Word

Bearer said.

The mob surged forward.

I threw Harrison to the ground.

I whipped out my sword.

The mob came.

They swung.

They punched.

They kicked.

I slashed and lashed at them.

Fingers sliced.

Arms hacked to pieces.

Chests slaughtered.

Corpses fell to the ground.

Then it stopped.

It all stopped as the air started to crackle loudly. Bright lightning zapped the mob back.

Harrison tapped my ankle, and I knew what he was looking at.

"Dearest Daniel Fireheart, it is so good to see you. It is good to be home," Fateweaver said.

CHAPTER 13

Standing behind a thick rough tree, its massive branches rustling in the cold afternoon breeze, Alessandria watched the mob in all their different shapes, sizes and classes massing outside the Fortress of the Inquisitorial Order of the Divine Air.

The mob shouted and screamed at the Fortress. Alessandria shook her head at how silly these people were being.

The Fortress itself was unbelievable. But Alessandria knew it would be unbelievable if she didn't know too much about the Inquisition. Yet after learning so much and seeing their cruelly and unique ways for herself. Nothing about that damned organisation surprised her anymore.

Looking at the Fortress, Alessandria frowned ad she looked at the massive solid walls covered in bright blinding features. It was like some artist had wiped a paint brush across the Fortress. Bright vibrant blue, pink, red and orange feathers coated the walls in a thick layer. There was something strangely hypnotic about it but Alessandria turned away.

Turning her attention to the mob, there must have been hundreds of them. Judging by the dirty, sweaty smell of them it could have been more but Alessandria couldn't see past the brow of the Hill.

For some reason the Inquisition had destroyed their own bridge, Alessandria wasn't sure why. But at least that would buy the Order time to react and hopefully attack.

She wasn't exactly sure why Nemesio had wanted to come here instead of heading to the Grande Cathedral. Maybe he wanted to get some allies to help protect the now fortified House of the Gods. Smart. But Alessandria would still prefer to go to the Grande Cathedral and target Fateweaver.

After all if the Inquisition suffered then that was surely a good thing. No good had ever come from that organisation.

Then Alessandria turned her head to admire her stunning Nemesio in his red and blue fiery armour as he stood behind some trees. But something good had come out of the Inquisition. Something she would protect to the end.

Rolling her eyes, Alessandria knew she had to attempt to save this Order but there had to be a reason Nemesio wanted to come here.

Hellen stepped forward. Her grey Procurator cloaked giving her a respectable amount of camouflage in the trees. Her massive wooden stick looking just like another branch. (It probably was a branch)

Nemesio stepped forward. "We need to get in there. This Order has no secret passages I'm aware of,"

"Why are we here? The mob is focused on the

castle and here. The Grande Cathedral is less defended-"

"Beautiful, why would the enemy focus here? They would focus on the castle, kill the Queen and make sure Fateweaver rules. Why focus here?"

Alessandria smiled. "There's something here they want,"

"Or they wanna keep something in," Hellen said.

Alessandria nodded. It was clever, but why was this Order so dangerous to them? Thinking about what she knew of this Order, there was nothing special about them. Except their extreme devotion to birds.

Something moved in the trees.

Alessandria spun around.

Mobsters were coming.

Alessandria swore. She didn't need this.

They all grabbed their weapons.

Maybe the Order would see them and want to help them.

Alessandria looked at her friends. They nodded.

They charged.

Alessandria thrusted her sword into their backs.

Sword slicing through flesh and bone.

Blood sprayed out.

Alessandria slashed her sword in long bloody arcs.

The mob was alert now.

They spun.

Hellen charged over.

Whacking her stick wildly.

Bones crunched.

Bones shattered.

Bones crushed.

Nemesio stormed forward.

Slashing and lashing with rage.

His sword chomped on flesh.

Massive chunks of flesh fell to the ground.

Alessandria hacked away at the mob.

Heads rolled on the ground.

The mob was very alert now.

They all charged forward.

Alessandria jumped back.

The mob ran at them.

Alessandria stood firm.

Her blade swirled rapidly.

Slicing deep into unarmed flesh.

Dark red blood sprayed everywhere.

The mob kept coming.

Hellen whacked the mob.

It didn't stop them.

Nemesio thrusted his sword into the mobsters.

Corpses collapsed to the ground.

It didn't matter.

The mob kept coming.

Alessandria looked at the feather covered Fortress.

No one was there.

This was a stupid idea.

The mob slapped Alessandria.

She fell to the ground.

Hands reached out.

Hellen screamed.

Alessandria needed to get to her.

Hellen screamed loudly.

Nemesio was silent.

Hands grabbed Alessandria.

Pulling at her arms.

Pulling at her ears.

She screamed in agony.

Heat washed over her.

Alessandria punched the hands away.

More hands came.

They wrapped around her throat.

They squeezed.

Her lungs gasped for air.

Alessandria wanted to scream.

She couldn't.

She didn't have enough air.

Vision turned to black.

Alessandria could see a ghostly form of her Mother.

This wasn't happening.

Alessandria struggled.

It was useless.

Something shrieked.

The mob stopped.

They let go.

A deafening choir of shrieking birds filled the air.

Alessandria couldn't see anything.

A massive bird shot down.

Talons skewering the mobsters.

Alessandria got to the ground.

More massive birds shot down.

They all shrieked.

Their talons slashed the throats of the enemy.

The birds grabbed the mobsters.

Clawfuls at a time.

The birds flew high.

Then dropped them.

The mobsters cracked on the ground.

Chunks of blood, muscles and bones rained down.

Then nothing.

Alessandria looked up into the sky.

Twenty birds flew towards her.

She went to grab her sword.

She couldn't find it.

The birds flew down.

Then… they transformed.

Alessandria blinked and there were twenty Inquisitors wearing a long pink, red and orange feathered cloak.

Looking around in confusion, Alessandria saw Hellen and Nemesio thankfully okay as they inspected the Inquisitors. This was strange. Humans turning into birds and back again. She had heard crazy stories from her Father in the past but this was taking it a bit too far. Surely?

The sound of iron shrieking against stone made

Alessandria cover her ears as she looked to see the massive iron gate of the Fortress open.

All the Inquisitors looked at Alessandria and pointed towards the gate. They obviously wanted her and her friends, but what was going on here?

CHAPTER 14

Turning around I was expecting to see Fateweaver standing there with the mob of all different people of different sizes and classes smiling at him. But when I turned around to look at whatever had spoken to me. There was nothing.

All I saw were the angry faces of the mind controlled mobsters with the massive gold walls behind them depicting amazing battles from our history and moments. And the massive black mouldy sheets of silk hanging loosely on the walls.

The mob moaning and making strange inhuman noises.

My dulled blade spun slowly as I looked at the mob. I supposed this was the first time I had actually had an opportunity to see them up close.

They were definitely mind controlled.

Their eyes weren't life filled and vivid with their pupils constantly reacting to the changing light in the throne room. Instead their eyes were dead, glassy and some of them looked as if their eyes were made from part boiled eggs.

I didn't want this. This was awful, and I wasn't even referring to the smell of something strange. It wasn't the normal sweat and dirt coming from the mob. It was something else entirely. The smell was definitely chemical with a hint of cinnamon and dried herbs.

Then I remembered the smell, it was years ago and I had 'borrowed' one of Alessandria's copies of Procurator Times. There was a case of a Cult in there that used a drug mixture to make their members compliant. And it smelt like chemicals with cinnamon and dried herbs.

Whilst a part of me fancied a nice cinnamon bun, I turned my attention to the love of my life. My beautiful Harrison, how badly I wanted to will him away from this danger. I felt as if I had failed him in some way as he sat there. His beautiful longish blond hair messy and him looking at his legs. Probably willing them to move. I don't blame him, but I love him no matter what.

The sound of the Queen tapping her feet made me look at her and the Word Bearer. The Queen looked furious at the Word Bearer as he sat there in his long white robes and his youthful face and features. Despite him being close to 90.

A part of me felt sorry for the throne, having to cope with having that horrid man sit on it. It was probably for the best it wasn't living. But if it wasn't living then how was it being corrupted? The gold was still turning black and flaky and the jewels were still falling off.

I turned to the Word Bearer. "Why?"

"Why what little gay?"

"Why do this all? You claim it is in the name of Gods and Goddesses to serve a higher power. But I know the truth,"

"Gays and your fellow abominations know nothing. You're a disease-"

I waved him silent. He seemed shocked.

"These are the words of a puppet. Not a Master," I said.

He shook his head.

"I do all of this because it is the Fate of the Church,"

I knew Fateweaver was using him. That was simple. The hard part was making Fateweaver come out.

"Fate? The Gods design your Fate. The Fate of the religion rests on their being a Monarch and a Church as two separate beings," I said.

He shook his head violently.

The Queen smiled.

"It is my Fate to rule over these common diseased people. You have diseased their minds into thinking your kind is okay,"

As he was talking I realised for the first time, I didn't care what words he was saying. I was gay and autistic. I was happy with both. I loved being gay and autistic. So if he hated me that didn't matter. I was more than confident in who I was.

Now I needed to focus on my mission and kill Fateweaver, and I had a fairly good idea about how to do that.

"But you don't think that do you Word Bearer? You Bear the Words. But who's Words?"

The Word Bearer cocked his head.

The mob muttered around me.

"I Bear the Words of the Gods and Goddesses. I-"

"You Bear the Words of One God, don't you? The God of Fate. The Weaver of Fate,"

His face froze.

A part of me would hate to see inside his mind to see all the emotional hate going on inside him. He was a traitor to his own Church. No worshipper would ever preach the words of one God let alone a False god. There was no God of Fate.

The Queen whipped out her blade and walked over to the Word Bearer who was crying.

His entire world was crumbling around him. The air crackled with blue lightning but it didn't seem like anyone else could see it.

The Queen thrusted her sword into the Word Bearer.

But the blade stopped.

It stopped a centimetre from his chest.

Blue lightning wrapped around her.

I charged forward.

My sword raised.

Harrison screamed.

I stopped and spun.

He was screaming.

Dark blue lightning wrapped around his throat.

I needed to choose.

It was too late.

The Queen vomited.

Then my eyes widened as I saw her sword drop to the ground and her other sword floated out of its sheath. Both swords floated and landed next to the throne.

I wanted to rush over to the Queen but I knew it was too late. Her eyes were glassy and distant, and her armour turned black.

She sat cross-legged on the floor. Staring into space. Would that happen to Harrison? I spun around but Harrison was okay. The lightning was gone.

"More proof gays aren't intelligent," the Word Bearer said.

How I didn't attack him myself!

"What did you do?" I asked.

"I did nothing abomination. This is what you did. I have to cure her. I don't know how you corrupted her mind with the gay virus but I have to cure her for Ordericous. Soon Fateweaver will be here. She will be saved,"

Whilst I mostly ignored his words, I thought for just a second this was the real Word Bearer. Perhaps he was a good but utterly stupid man. Perhaps he really did want to do good but he believed there was a gay virus and the Word Bearer wanted to help save the country.

In all honesty, I hardly cared if he was good or not at heart. He had threatened me, my family, my Queen and most important the man I love too many times. He would die. I just needed patience.

CHAPTER 15

Even being here a second time was strange, Alessandria knew that as soon as the Inquisitor led them into the meeting chamber and left them.

The meeting chamber hadn't changed too much since before but it was just so strange. The walls were still covered in an impressive array of red, pink, blue and orange feathers that coated the walls thickly. Alessandria didn't know if she liked the feathers. They made the room interesting but it was an assault on the eyes. And all the feathers had a slight scent of lemon with a hint of cedarwood to them.

Moving her glare to the middle of the chamber that had changed. Alessandria cocked her head as she stared at the large pile of bird bones with a sort of small brown bird's nest on top.

Alessandria wanted to go over and inspect it but that might have been disrespectful. Then she thought about the Inquisitors being able to turn into birds. What if that was someone's bed?

Again she heard the shrieking of birds nearby. Before Alessandria had thought the Order trained birds but now, she didn't know. Did they train birds or did they train human birds?

Alessandria shook her head at the thought. Human birds. There had to be a better name for that surely.

The sound of Hellen tapping her massive wooden stick against the feather covered walls made Alessandria want to tell her to stop. But the idea of moaning at Hellen frightened her. Especially as it felt as if Hellen's time was limited. Alessandria knew she was just being paranoid.

Her beautiful Nemesio in his red and blue fiery armour paced around her before they all stopped as the door opened again. The Sage of the Order of the Divine Air walked in. His body looked different than before less defined and more fatigued. Even his long feather covered cloaked looked tired and aged.

Looking up at his face, Alessandria's eyes narrowed as she saw him wearing another bird skull. This time it was a massive Eagle of some kind. Definitely not native to Ordericous.

"We have to work together," he said, his voice harsh and rough.

"We wanted to work with you. We wanted your help," Alessandria said.

The Sage nodded. "I'm sorry but our secrets. Our abilities. Our... I don't know,"

Alessandria really looked at the Sage. He was so different from all the others. He wasn't an arrogant, extremist who wanted all the unholy to die. Alessandria saw him as a man who wanted to protect the country he loved and its citizens.

"Why are the mob here? Why target this place?" Nemesio asked.

The Sage tilted his head back. "Us. We're special, unique whatever you want to call us. Fateweaver is something to do with our history,"

Alessandria stepped forward. "Tell me everything,"

"Whenever we ascend to Sagehood we are given a book to read. If our Minds can survive reading it, we become a Sage,"

"What this book laddy?" Hellen asked.

"The dark truth of the Inquisition so-called Saint Bennett didn't make the Inquisition freely. Fateweaver made him. No one ever knows Fateweaver made them do anything,"

Alessandria nodded.

"When the Inquisition was broken up, a shard of Bennett's consciousness made the Divine Air a secret from Fateweaver. We were charged with finding and killing the Fateweaver Family,"

"My Father?" Alessandria asked.

"He came to us so many times. I don't know how he knew about us. He just did. He knew our secret history. I turned him away,"

"Why!" Alessandria shouted.

The Sage looked to the floor. "I don't know. Pride. A citizen did what the Inquisition could not,"

Alessandria spat at the Sage.

"I deserve that. I really do. My Order kept tabs on him. He did great. I'm sorry he died,"

"My Mother?"

The Sage probably smiled under his bird skull.

"Quite a woman. Yes she came but she wanted something very specific and she gave me very specific instructions,"

"That sounds like ya ma,"

Alessandria nodded.

"Your Mother wanted me not to do anything about Fateweaver. She demanded it,"

"No-"

"That's true Lady Alessandria," the Sage said.

Alessandria couldn't believe it.

"Then your Mother asked me to give her two things. The passage that you probably found in her hand and some plant to give her-"

"A heart attack," Alessandria said.

Nemesio hugged her.

"Ya Mother final scheme," Hellen said.

Alessandria laughed. Her Mother knew how to scheme and plot to the end.

"What else?" she asked.

"Not much else. She told me to turn you away when you first came. Then your Mother gave me two final demands,"

Alessandria placed a hand on his feather covered shoulders.

"Please tell me,"

"She demanded I take you through the secret tunnels into the castle. Then she demanded I explain the Loom of Fate,"

"Why we gonna find it in that Churchy?"

"Miss Hellen, you are mistaken. Lady Kinaaz Fireheart wanted to miss lead you. She needed you heading in this direction, and she knew the mob would throw you off. Then there's a probability Nemesio would lead you here,"

Nemesio shook his head. Alessandria kissed him.

"He lives in between all the lives of us and he rests in front of the Loom of Fates. Falling asleep as he weaves the Loom," the Sage said.

"Where?" Alessandria asked.

"There's a chamber in the Castle. A very old and some say haunted chamber in the castle. The tunnel leads you straight to it then the throne room is close by,"

"And the Loom is in there and we can kill Fateweaver," Alessandria said, her excitement building.

"Not quite. Kill the Loom and Fateweaver can't Weave the Fates anymore but he's still dangerous,"

Alessandria stepped away and hugged both Nemesio and Hellen. It felt like they were nearing the climax. A do or die moment. Alessandria didn't want anything to happen to them.

The Sage let out an almighty bird cry.

"Come on," the Sage said as he opened a gap in the wall. Tens of Inquisitors already there waiting. "We fight for the freedom of the world today,"

CHAPTER 16

I really hated the Word Bearer. He looked so stupid in his long white perfect robes with his false youthful face and perfect features. He was clearly using some kind of magic but it was silly.

Even the throne seemed to agree with me as more of the former gold turned pitch black and flaked off. More precious gems fell onto the floor.

My dulled blade turned slowly as I started to notice even the bright golden walls, showing the mighty depictions of grand battles and moments in Ordericousian history, started to look decayed. Black spots stained the gold and some of it started to fall off.

The chemical smell with a hint of dried herbs and cinnamon grew stronger now (I still wanted a cinnamon roll as the taste formed on my tongue) and the mob of people tightly packed into the throne room moaned. Their eyes glassy and lifeless.

Looking over at the Queen, she still sat cross-legged and dazed. Her eyes were so distant and glassy. I wanted to do something but I didn't know what. I needed Fateweaver to come out and if that failed I needed to buy time until Alessandria got here. Together we could and would stop this.

I heard Harrison moan as he rolled himself over to me. Looking back I saw a group of mobsters stroking the air as if he was still there. Their eyes were like hard boiled eggs. I wanted to feel sorry for them but the symbol round their necks told me they were extreme nuns. I couldn't feel sorry for people who caned little girls for laughing and wanting to be children.

Kneeling down (and because I wanted to annoy the Word Bearer) I pressed my beautiful Harrison's body against mine. His smooth soft hands wrapped in mine and my mouth buried itself in his perfect longish blond hair. I kissed his head.

The Word Bearer jumped up.

"Stop that! This is unholy-"

The Word Bearer wanted to continue but his tongue melted. Bright red and pink liquid poured down this chest. He tried to scream but strange animal noises came out.

"Be silent and stop your stupid preaching," something said.

I didn't recognise the voice but it was wise, harsh and very unfriendly.

Looking around, my eyes locked on a figure who appeared a few metres from me. I didn't know what this thing was. Its long humanoid limbs were covered in thick black and red scales, long sharp talons replaced fingers and toes.

What shocked me more were the two long blue wings covered in sharp metallic feathers. Then I looked at his face. I wish I hadn't. Its face was of a bird, a long sharp bright blue beak with short blue feathers covered its entire body.

Whatever this thing was it smelt fresh and clean. Like a spring morning or something like that. I don't know. This was strange to me.

The last thing I noticed was the creature held a long golden staff in its hand. Nothing special. Just a rod of gold but it made the air hum gently with magical energy.

"Fateweaver," I said, quietly.

The Word Bearer tried to talk but only loud deformed noises came out.

"Daniel Fireheart. You have changed. You are stronger now. I can sense it. Your soul and will are stronger. This one," Fateweaver said, pointing the gold staff at Harrison.

I pulled Harrison closer.

"Relax Daniel Fireheart I have no desire to hurt Harrison. I will kill him in the end. Before I kill you. But he is safe for now,"

I spat at him.

"Daniel Fireheart that is most ungrateful. I have silenced the Word Bearer for you,"

I had no idea if that was meant to make me happy or not. Granted it was better that the Word Bearer couldn't call me names anymore.

"Why come out now?" I asked.

Fateweaver opened his beak. Revealing thousands of layers of tiny razor sharp teeth.

"That Word Bearer was boring me Daniel Fireheart. I couldn't listen to any more homophobic talk. He needed to get a life,"

I had to smile at that.

"You murdered my Father,"

Fateweaver seemed surprised I had changed the conversation so quickly.

"Self-defence. Your Father was a pain. I killed him, Daniel Fireheart,"

I wanted to jump out and kill him, but I needed Alessandria here first. And what was the endgame?

"I will admit Daniel Fireheart your Father was a clever man. I tried for years to weave your fate and the Fate of your family. I cannot. Your Father was a pain like that,"

Fateweaver walked over to the Queen. The Queen seemed to smile at his presence. Her eyes became even more distant and lifeless.

"But you. You were touchable. Not at first. Daniel Fireheart your Father probably tried to protect her. Not well enough. She is mine,"

I helped Harrison onto the ground softly. Then I stood up.

"She is not yours!" I shouted.

He laughed. His beak making it more of a rough crackle than a true laugh.

"Daniel Fireheart, I can kill you and Harrison now with a single thought. But your Father's protection is still strong on you both. I need to weaken it,"

My heart beated faster.

"My endgame is simple-" Fateweaver said.

I stepped forward. "You want to do the Binding Ritual. It won't work. It's a myth,"

"You really are stupid. In theory it's a myth. In reality Daniel Fireheart, it works," Fateweaver said, gesturing to the hundreds of mind controlled mobsters in the throne room.

I knew there were even more outside.

"All these mortals. All these stupid worshippers, Daniel Fireheart. They worship the Queen as a Goddess. The Living Embodiment of the Gods. Of course she isn't. But these people believe it. They pray to her,"

My stomach churned as he spoke.

"All their emotions and wishes and dreams, Daniel Fireheart coalescent into her soul. She had more magic and power within her than she'll ever realise," Fateweaver said.

I didn't know what to say or do. I don't even know how Fateweaver would hope to extract this so-called magic within her.

I whipped out my sword.

I charged forward.

Fateweaver crackled.

He slammed his staff onto the ground.

I froze. My muscles and bones wanted to move but I couldn't. My body floated over to Harrison. He too was frozen. That was too far.

Fateweaver cocked his head. Looking at me but I

didn't feel like he was looking at me. But what I represented.

He swirled his hand. The shadowy demon formed in front of Fateweaver. Its humanoid shadowy form crackling and flashing with magical energy.

"Alessandria and her friends are in the tunnel. Kill them all,"

CHAPTER 17

Alessandria's feet splashed cold water up her leather booted legs as she walked through the dark grey stone tunnel. The light from torches flickering wildly as they all walked through the tunnels. Giving the tunnel a faint smell of smoke.

The cobblestone floor of the tunnels were rough and chipped from centuries of ageing. Alessandria had no idea if anyone had been down here in that time. Maybe they had. Maybe they hadn't. There was no way to tell.

Despite it being a late autumn afternoon, the tunnels were freezing down here. Alessandria could feel the hairs on her arms stand up.

Hellen had already wrapped her grey Procurator cloaked round herself tightly and her massive wooden stick had a slight shake as it moved. Perhaps Hellen was shivering.

The sound of feet splashing in the puddles quietly echoed around the tunnel. Alessandria knew the entire Inquisitorial Order of the Divine Air had joined them on their mission.

In all honesty, Alessandria didn't know whether to be humbled or not. She remembered her history lessons from her childhood and there was no mention of an entire Order marching before. But having the country taken over by the church hadn't happened before.

All the Inquisitors in their bright feathered cloaks held their swords by their waists whilst they talked amongst themselves. Alessandria tried to listen but it sounded like they were speaking Ordericousian and bird song. There was a tweet or several after every human word. Strange.

Looking ahead the tunnel seemed to go on forever then Alessandria looked down a little. To see her stunning Nemesio in that wonderful red and blue fiery armour with that long perfect hair. She wanted to run her hand through it but this wasn't the time.

Alessandria saw him talking to the Sage of the Order. They had been talking for at least an hour. From what Alessandria could make out. (They spoke mainly in Inquisitorial code) they were catching up on what the Inquisition was like, what had changed and their past experiences.

Then Alessandria thought about Daniel, her amazing brother who could defy all the odds. She knew something was wrong. It was a strange sibling sense. He needed her. Everyone needed her. Alessandria couldn't fail and that's what scared her.

The Inquisitors stopped.

Alessandria and Hellen did too.

All the Inquisitors swords glowed dark red.

Alessandria didn't know what that meant. She had seen it before. It was like the Queen's swords.

Screams filled the tunnels.

The Inquisitors turned into little birds.

They screamed.

They shrieked.

They didn't want this.

The little birds fell to the ground.

These birds were too small.

They couldn't support a living human.

The Sage flashed.

Whatever was happening here. It didn't work on him.

He whipped out his swords.

Alessandria and co did the same.

Little bird corpses covered the floor.

Tens of dark red glowing swords littered the floor.

The hairs on Alessandria's neck stood up.

Something was here.

They weren't alone.

The air hummed with magical power.

Something moved in the shadows.

Something jumped out.

Alessandria swung.

Her sword melted.

A shadowy hand grabbed her throat.

Alessandria didn't care.

She stared at the demon. Its shadowy form an assault on her eyes. She hated it.

Hellen charged forward.

Whacking the demon.

The demon dropped Alessandria.

Hellen whacked the demon again.

The Sage charged.

The demon shrieked.

It disappeared.

Nemesio swung his sword behind him.

The demon screamed.

Something at the back of Alessandria's mind kicked her. She knew how to kill it. She couldn't remember for now.

Torches blew out.

The glowing swords covered everything in a red glow.

A shadow climbed on the walls.

Alessandria grabbed a red sword.

She swung it.

She missed.

The demon slammed its fists into her back.

Alessandria fell forward.

Crushing the little bird corpses.

The demon shrieked.

Why?

Why shriek at the little birds?

The demon flew at her.

Alessandria swung again.

Hellen whacked the demon.

Nemesio sliced into the demon.

Each hit made it laugh.

The Sage was frozen.

The air hummed loudly around him.

Alessandria stomped on a little corpse.

The bird corpse shattered.

The demon flickered.

Alessandria slashed and lashed at the little corpses.

The demon shrieked.

She didn't know what was happening.

She didn't care.

The air crackled with magical energy.

Hellen and Nemesio saw what she was doing. They joined her.

The little bird bodies popped.

The demon charged forward.

Alessandria didn't care.

She stomped on the final little bird body. The demon stopped and laughed. Then Alessandria stopped and realised what she had done.

The Sage stepped forward. "You idiots. They were my friends. They were still alive. The demon tricked you. If you killed him they would turn back,"

Nemesio and Hellen looked at each other, their eyes wet and wide. Alessandria cocked her head. She didn't understand magic in a lot of its complexities but that wasn't right.

Pulling on her limited magical power, Alessandria focused on the Sage. She needed to see if he was lying knowingly or not. Alessandria's eyes were fixed on him. She bore into his soul.

The Sage and all his secrets and lies and half truths. Then Alessandria saw his beliefs on what he had just said. He thought he was telling the truth, but he wasn't. Alessandria knew he had been lied to.

Alessandria shook her head. "You were lied to…"

She was about to continue when she remembered what the demon was. Alessandria had found the demon's name mentioned in one page in the *Complete History of Ordericous.*

Alessandria smiled and looked at Nemesio and Hellen. "Be ready,"

They nodded.

"Atarangi," Alessandria said.

The air crackled and pulsed with bright red magic. Lightning bolts chipped and exploded some of the stone walls. But moments later a humanoid shape started to form.

A few seconds later, a creature with long elongated limbs covered in thick oily red scales formed. Its head still covered in shadow.

"Atarangi, you're done," Alessandria said.

Hellen and Nemesio swung.

Hellen whacked Atarangi in the head.

Nemesio sliced into its flesh.

Shadowy black blood poured from the demon.

Atarangi stormed forward.

Jumping on Alessandria.

Her skin burnt.

Smoke poured off her.

She screamed in agony.

Hellen went to attack.

Atarangi waved Hellen away.

Hellen slammed into a wall.

Nemesio grabbed Atarangi.

His hand burnt.

Atarangi waved Nemesio away.

Alessandria screamed again.

The pain was unreal.

Every cell in her body screamed.

The Sage charged.

Ripping off his bird helmet.

Atarangi screamed in terror.

Alessandria understood.

The Sage was no human.

Its head was unnatural. A constant moving mass of flesh. Millions of bird faces moved and screamed as one.

Alessandria went to scream but nothing came out.

The Sage grabbed Atarangi.

The Sage's hands turned to talons.

It ripped chunks of flesh out of Atarangi.

The Sage's face covered Atarangi's.

Alessandria needed to scream.

The Sage absorbed Atarangi into itself.

The Demon gave a final horrific scream before it died.

Alessandria's body relaxed. No pain was left inside her.

Even stranger the Sage lumped against one of the stone walls as he fell to the ground. Alessandria crawled over to him. His face a horrible thing to look at. So many bird faces screaming and shrieking in eternal torment.

Alessandria bravely touched his talons.

"Don't be afraid. I won't hurt you," he said, clearly in agony.

Alessandria didn't know what to say.

"Your Mother a clever woman. She didn't care about Fateweaver for now. She wanted you to get my support,"

Alessandria smiled. Her Mother was always unpredictable.

"She loved that damn brother of yours,"

Hellen and Nemesio walked over.

The Sage grabbed Alessandria's hand and forced his seal into it.

"Here have your pledge. You and that brother deserve it. Destroy the Church. Make Ordericous great and equal,"

Alessandria nodded. She would make it a place where everyone could be free.

The Sage stroked her face weakly. "Your Mother said a final thing. She got you this far. The rest is in you and your Brother's hands. You're never alone and she loves you so much,"

The Sage turned into a pile of little bird corpses that turned to dust.

CHAPTER 18

My muscles were stiff as the magic from Fateweaver's staff continued to hold me. It felt like a bodybuilder was holding you. I didn't enjoy this. At least Fateweaver had been 'kind' enough to allow me to move my head.

The corruption was definitely growing, I realised as I looked around. The long black mouldy sheets of silk were frayed so badly massive holes littered the sheets.

My suspicions about the gold walls, with all their amazing depictions of battles and vital historical moments, were clearly correct. Great streaks of black shot up them. It was like someone had grabbed a paintbrush and stroked the walls with it. Little amounts of black gold fell off as the golden walls turned flaky and died.

The sound of the Word Bearer and the mind controlled mob was awful. Their loud moaning animal noises were disgusting.

My dulled blade was frozen in my hand. I wanted to turn it but Fateweaver must have known I needed it to stay calm. Maybe that's why he let me keep it.

The smell of chemicals with hints of cinnamon and dried herbs was weaker now. Being replaced with the smell of rotten meat and sweet frankincense.

Turning my attention to Fateweaver, I cocked my head and my eyes narrowed. His long red scaly limbs and talons were fingers and toes should have been were strange. They were drawing weird symbols on the floor that busted into crimson flames when they were done. That was all outside another shape.

This other shape was some kind of pentagram with the Queen sitting in the middle. She sat there smiling. Her eyes were still dead and they started to look cooked. I needed to act now. I just hoped my beautiful Harrison was okay. But I really needed my sister here.

I had to buy more time.

"Your Majesty listen to my voice. Look at me!" I shouted.

She didn't. The Queen just continued to sit there in the pentagram.

"Isabella," I said.

The Queen seemed to register the name. Her eyes became softer and more life filled.

"Isabella listen to me. Fight this. I know you can. I believe in you!"

Pain flooded my body. Harrison screamed in agony. My limbs twisted in strange directions.

The Queen's eyes turned distant and lifeless. The pain stopped but I hoped I had done enough.

Fateweaver looked at me after he finished another symbol that busted crimson flames.

"I admire you for that. It was brave. Stupid but

brave, Daniel Fireheart. Your Queen is mine,"

Feeling something within my mind click, I felt as if I could move a finger. I had no idea what my autistic mind was doing but it had defeated Fateweaver's mother. Hopefully I could defeat his mind trick. I just needed time.

"Isabella is stronger than you know. She is a Queen, a Goddess. Her people love her," I said.

Fateweaver nodded. "Daniel Fireheart that is what made it all so easy. It was simple to convince the Word Bearer here to attack the Queen out of love,"

The Word Bearer made a sound. Maybe he was protesting his innocence or something. It didn't matter.

"Then once I controlled him. His worshippers followed. I didn't need to do many of my normal tricks to weave this Fate, dear Daniel Fireheart,"

"Is this really all so you can just kill me and my family?" I asked.

He seemed a bit confused by the question. I'm not sure he even knew why he was doing this anymore.

"The Fateweavers Weave the Fate of the world. Your family prevented us from conquering the world years ago. I am here for revenge. My brothers and sisters murdered by your Father. Daniel Fireheart, Kinaaz Fireheart and Alessandria Fireheart will all die,"

I cocked my head. "Where is my Mother?"

Of course I knew the answer but I'm not sure if

he did.

Fateweaver smiled. "Daniel Fireheart I do not know but when I do-"

I laughed at him. I really laughed so did Harrison.

"My Mother is dead," I said.

Fateweaver looked horrified. A lot of things became clear for me.

"She beat you. You weaved her Fate or tried to and she denied it. She killed herself. She must have. All in an elaborate plan to kill you. Yes, yea that's it. My Mother was clever. She would make Alessandria think her plan was to get support for the law change,"

Fateweaver's beak snarled.

"My Mother always wanted to kill you. That was her final scheme,"

The mob moaned and made panicked animal noises.

"Daniel Fireheart, you forget I am free. You are not,"

I smiled. For some reason I just knew I could break free now. But I wanted to wait.

Fateweaver finished a symbol in the shape of some kind of eye and he sat in the middle of the pentagram. The Queen smiled as he sat next to her.

The Word Bearer moaned and tried to scream in protest. I knew what was going to happen. I didn't expect the how.

Fateweaver swirled his staff in the air.

The Word Bearer tried to scream but droplets of red liquid poured off his skin. Bright red drops of something fell onto the ground.

Looking at the Word Bearer, I realised these red droplets were his skin, muscles and bones.

Each drop revealed more of his flesh and body.

He screamed in agony as his body melted.

Within seconds his entire body splashed onto the floor. His face melted last and the image of him screaming in utter terror will forever be engrained into my memory. At least in death that idiot would know how my people felt as he pointlessly killed them.

The air crackled with magical energy.

Bright red lightning shot around the throne room.

The Queen smiled.

Fateweaver's beak opened.

His long bird like tongue shot into the Queen's mouth.

She laughed in delight.

Her skin paled.

He was doing something.

The lightning got fierce.

The throne exploded.

Turning to ash.

I needed to act.

Breaking free. I charged forward.

I was free.

I was ready to kill him.

CHAPTER 19

Alessandria closed the massive cold wooden door as her, her stunning Nemesio and Hellen walked into an ancient stone storage room.

She couldn't explain it but it was a sixth sense had led her from the tunnel to here. Thankfully because of whatever was going on with the Queen and Daniel, the castle was mainly empty.

Alessandria coughed as a thick layer of dust covered her skin and the smell of musty old parchment filled her nose.

Looking around she shook her head at all the rubbish in here. The chamber itself could make for a great dining room. The domed stone ceiling looked impressive as did the hard cold red stone bricks that made up the walls.

Instead some wise person in the castle had decided to make it a storage room. All around Alessandria there were piles upon piles of forgotten things. Next to her was a pile of mouldy books and other legal documents.

As a Dominicus Procurator, she was horrified. All legal documents are vital so the thought of someone abandoning them sickened her.

Hellen moved some old furniture and children toys with her massive wooden stick. Her grey Procurator cloaked already caked in dust.

Alessandria couldn't blame her friend. It was a mess in here. But there was a massive perfectly formed pile of broken looms, clothes and other textile related things in the middle of the storage room.

It was the kind of pile you would expect if someone had placed an object in the middle they wanted to hide.

Walking over to it, Alessandria covered her nose as the musty smell grew in intensity. She moved a few pieces of broken loom, the pieces feeling rough and unloved in her hands.

Hellen and beautiful Nemesio came over and helped. After moving more junk and rubbish. Including plenty of moth-eaten clothes. The rest of the pile fell away.

Revealing their target, Alessandria gave a massive smile as she admired the smooth, perfectly intact wood and the impressive array of glowing threads of cotton on the loom. The threads were wrapped and weaved perfectly. They formed a strong looking sheet of cotton but Alessandria sensed something.

She wasn't sure if Nemesio and Hellen could see it but some of the threads were pulsing brightly. And on every thread, there was a little white light. Presumably someone's soul travelling towards their Fate.

Some of the lights were close to the right of the loom. Lots were to the left. Presumably the threads of

Fate went left to right but this was still amazing to see.

Hellen stepped closer. She raised her massive wooden stick.

Alessandria went to stop her. It was too late.

Hellen whacked it. A burst of magical energy flew her across the room.

The air hummed with magical energy and something stepped out of the loom.

It was something strangely humanoid. It wasn't made from flesh and bone but crackling magical energy. The thing's red skin was unhealthy and thin. The creature was hunched.

Alessandria stared at its face. The strange triangular nature of it reminded her of bedtime stories. Those two black abysses for eyes weren't right. But two long fangs hung out of its mouth.

The creature looked at Alessandria. Those black abysses seemed to darken even further.

"Alessandria Fireheart," the Creature said, its voice strained like it was learning how to speak.

Alessandria smiled. She had a feeling who it was from what Daniel told her.

"Fateweaver Primus or a shard of that foul thing," Alessandria said.

Primus seemed to nod and give Alessandria something like a smile but it wasn't. It was deformed and twisted.

"You cannot kill the Loom. If my Loom dies then my son cannot regenerate,"

"If ya Loom that good missy. What happened to the rest of ya children?" Hellen said.

Primus paused. She didn't know. Maybe her true self did but this little shard of consciousness and power had no idea.

Alessandria whipped out her sword.

Primus shook her head. She reared back.

Nemesio, Hellen and Alessandria charged.

They swung their swords.

Primus shrieked.

Hellen whacked her.

Primus screamed.

Alessandria covered her bleeding ears.

Primus waved her hand.

Hellen flew back.

Her head whacking into a pile of junk.

Nemesio dived out the way.

Primus' eyes glowed red.

The air crackled and hummed loudly.

It was like a thunderstorm.

Massive crashes of thunder filled the room.

Alessandria charged.

Lightning bolts hammered the floor.

Alessandria dodged them.

Primus went to attack.

Nemesio charged.

Primus turned.

She threw a lightning bolt.

It slammed into Nemesio.

It exploded.

Nemesio flew into a wall.

He was out.

Alessandria dodged more lightning bolts.

The little lights on the Loom flashed.

Millions of lights zoomed to the right.

So many lives about to die.

Alessandria stopped.

The lights moved back to the left. Alessandria focused on Primus who was still in battle mode. Fateweaver Primus launched a horrific lightning bolt at where Alessandria could have been standing if she had continued.

Primus still hadn't realised she was standing there.

Looking back over at the Loom, the little lights started to gently move towards the right. She needed to move. Alessandria needed to attack.

She charged.

Primus was distracted.

Nemesio regained consciousness.

He shouted and screamed at Primus.

Primus turned.

Magical energy thundering around her.

Primus launched her attack.

Alessandria kept charging.

Massive bolts of lightning screamed towards Nemesio.

All the junks and rubbish in the room lifted up.

It floated in the air.

The junk zoomed towards Nemesio.

Alessandria gasped.

Primus turned.

Alessandria was so close.

Primus tried to react.

Alessandria thrusted her sword into Primus.

Primus shrieked.

She slapped Alessandria away.

The air hummed again.

Lightning crackled around Alessandria.

Hellen whacked Primus in the head.

Her bones shattered.

The magic and lightning stopped.

Nemesio, Alessandria and Hellen didn't hesitate.

They charged towards the Loom.

Alessandria and Nemesio slashed and lashed the Loom.

Hellen whacked the Loom.

It shattered. Chunks of the Loom turned to dust but Alessandria smiled as she saw the little lights zoom across the Threads of Fate to the left.

CHAPTER 20

As The ritual started I knew I needed to act. The awful Fateweaver with his blue wings and face of a bird with that horrific beak sat there in the middle of the pentagram. With the strange crimson flaming symbols around it.

Fateweaver's long bird tongue shot into the Queen's mouth and she didn't care. This was all wrong. My mind needed to break free from this frozen prison.

My dulled blade twitched in my hand. I wanted to spin it rapidly. But I knew the mob of these mind controlled people with their eyes like hard boiled eggs would attack.

They still smelt of chemicals with awful hints of cinnamon and dried herbs.

Even now those mobsters still made animal noises as they presumably tried to cheer Fateweaver on. It was disgraceful.

All I wanted to do was kill everyone in this room, except my handsome Harrison and the Queen of course.

I wanted to get a torch and burn all these bright corrupted golden walls with their almighty depictions of battles and important moments. As for those long decaying black sheets of silks. I wanted to burn them.

My Flesheater ability twitched to be activated. I couldn't. Not till Alessandria was here.

My mind broke free.

I charged.

Whipping out my sword.

Fateweaver didn't see me.

The mob surged forward.

Harrison grunted.

I spun.

He whipped out his dagger.

He thrusted his dagger into the feet and legs of the mobsters.

The mobsters fell.

Harrison slit their throats.

I swung my blade.

This was a massacre.

Mobsters died in the tens.

My powerful sword swings sliced deep into flesh.

The mobsters' uncontrolled.

Their movements rough and sloppy.

They didn't know how to attack.

My blade slashed and lashed at their chests and faces.

I sliced into their hard-boiled egg eyes.

They didn't care.

They didn't feel it.

Harrison kept stabbing and thrusting.

The mobsters kept falling.

He was protecting.

My legs shot through a mobster.

Even their flesh was weak.

They weren't going to survive this.

The mob stopped.

I didn't.

I spun around.

Fateweaver was missing.

Fists slammed into my back.

I didn't move.

I swung my sword.

Fateweaver laughed.

He slapped my face.

He appeared in front of me.

He swung his staff.

I met it.

Magical energy crackled around us.

The air hummed in frustration.

No one wanted this.

I saw Harrison start to crawl.

I didn't want him to get hurt.

Fateweaver unleashed an onslaught of swings.

I struggled to dodge them.

My hand ached with each hit.

Fateweaver's attacks were powerful.

He kicked me.

Pain flooded my stomach.

I whacked him.

His staff buzzed and zapped the air.

I grabbed it.

It was stupid.

Images of death, pain and agony filled my mind.

Fateweaver panicked.

He punched me.

The staff pressed against my mind.

It wanted to control me.

Fateweaver didn't.

Fateweaver tried to pull the staff away.

The staff didn't let go of me.

Fateweaver shouted something.

I couldn't hear it.

Fateweaver screamed.

The staff released me.

Fateweaver kicked Harrison in the head.

I lunged forward.

Wrapping my hands around his throat.

How dare he!

His throat felt strange.

The feathers felt unnatural.

I squeezed.

No one attacks my Harrison.

Someone whacked me from behind.

I fell to the ground and Fateweaver started laughing manically. My first priority was always the man I loved. His nose was bleeding but he was okay. My beautiful Harrison was living proof that paralysed people were capable of amazing things. Without him I hate to think what the staff would have done to me.

Raising my head, I looked in utter horror as I saw

Fateweaver kissing the Queen lovingly. The way his beak moved was unnatural. A beak shouldn't move like a human mouth. But it did. This wasn't right.

Then it dawned on me that the Queen was the one who attacked me. Fateweaver or maybe the staff had control over her. Probably the Staff. Why else would Fateweaver not want me to be controlled?

There was much more to this than I knew about but this wasn't helping.

Standing back up I glared at Fateweaver, I went to step forward but ten mobsters grabbed me.

No. No. No. I hate touching, this was ridiculous. I hate touching!

My autism went into overdrive. The touching. No!

I forced myself not to lose control. I really wouldn't activate the Flesheater ability. Not now. I'm not sure if my ability would tell the Queen was not to be killed.

I took my dulled blade out of my pocket and my eyes narrowed at Fateweaver. He knew I would activate my ability if I needed to. If he threatened Harrison again, I would. I don't care about killing an old friend if Harrison is okay.

Fateweaver nodded and I spun my dulled blade slowly in my hand. Judging my Fateweaver's bird face I think he was concerned about the speed at which I spun.

Granted I'm useless or next to useless about reading emotions. I think he knew I wasn't scared or panicked. I knew his end was about to happen.

Guessing he was trying to get his mind off my dulled blade, he returned to the ritual and that horrific bird tongue shot back into the Queen. The air crackled violently. The climax wasn't far away now.

CHAPTER 21

Peaking round the corner of a massive stone corridor, Alessandria looked at the impressive stone corridor ahead that led to the throne room. Since leaving the storage room with the Loom, all Alessandria had seen was plain stone corridor after corridor.

Thankfully, this one had style. It was easily twenty metres long but every metre stood a black statue of an animal. Some were massive dogs with razor sharp teeth and others were of lions and tigers and elephants from far, far away countries. But in the middle of the corridor were five statues of massive men.

Even the floor looked pleasant with it being made from polish cast iron with diamonds and chunks of gold being suspended in it. It was amazing.

Alessandria coughed as the smell of charred ozone and strange chemicals with a faint hint of cinnamon and dried herbs filled the air.

Hellen started tapping Alessandria with her massive wooden stick as they both remembered the smell from Procurator Times. Alessandria nodded with certainty. She had expected mind control was being used to some extent. How else do you get thousands of worshippers to attack the Queen.

The sound of animal like moaning noises came from inside and Alessandria nodded. After reading the original story in the magazine, Alessandria had checked out some of the former cultists. They were all brain dead for the most part.

Fear gripped Alessandria as she thought about Daniel. Was he okay? Was he hurt? She needed to storm the throne room. He had to be in there.

Turning around to face her friends, Alessandria looked at Hellen in her grey Procurator cloak. Tapping her massive wooden stick in her hand. She wanted a fight. She wanted to save her country and protect Alessandria.

Then she looked at Nemesio her strong beautiful man in that amazing blue and red fiery armour.

Both of them nodded.

Alessandria turned back to look at the corridor and whipped out her sword. Her stomach churned it felt like someone was kicking inside.

Stepping out, Alessandria and co carefully walked down the corridor. The cast iron floor felt strangely warm against her leather booted feet.

Halfway down the corridor Alessandria heard her friends stop.

Turning around Alessandria saw Hellen inspecting the statues. Her friend's eyes were narrowing.

The statues moved.

They weren't statues.

They were five brutal men painted grey.

The brutes roared and screamed bloody murder.

Alessandria shook her head.

She didn't need this.

Her brother and her Queen were in danger.

Alessandria charged.

She was not muddying about.

She slammed his fists into a brutal.

The brutal didn't move.

She couldn't give a fuck.

Alessandria slashed the brutal with her sword.

A deep gash sliced into her chest.

Dark red rich blood poured out.

The brute went to punch Alessandria.

She still wasn't kidding about.

She swung her sword.

The brute grabbed it.

He snapped it.

Alessandria's rage calmed way down.

The brute grabbed her.

Throwing her against the wall.

He pressed against her.

Typical brute!

He smiled.

Alessandria slashed her nails across his face.

She slashed his eye.

She whacked him in between the legs.

The brute hesitated.

Hellen whacked him from behind.

The brute fell onto Alessandria.

She pulled him off.

Stomping on his head.

His skull cracked.

Four brutes left.

Another one charged into Hellen.

He grabbed Hellen.

He kept running.

Alessandria went to help.

A brute grabbed her wrist.

Alessandria relaxed.

She twisted herself free.

She went to punch the brute.

He grabbed her fists and squeezed.

Nemesio thrusted his sword into his back.

The brute didn't show pain.

He smiled.

The brute loved the pain.

Alessandria chomped on his hand.

He seemed scared.

Alessandria chomped harder.

Ripping a piece of flesh out.

Blood flooded her mouth.

The taste of iron was overwhelming.

The brute shrieked.

Alessandria jumped on him.

Wrapping her legs round his neck.

She squeezed.

By the gods she squeezed.

The brute turned blue.

Alessandria looked to Hellen.

Hellen snapped the neck of her brute.

The air roared.

Black shadows rose from the three corpses of the brutes.

The shadows were absorbed into the last two brutes.

Their bodies snapped and crushed as they grew.

Their skin being thicker.

Alessandria looked for a sword. Her half broken sword laid at her feet. She picked it up. She needed it.

The two brutes charged.

Their feet pounded into the ground.

Chipping and cracking the cast iron.

Alessandria went to dodge.

A brute grabbed her.

Nemesio slashed open the guts of one brute.

Fresh warm guts covered the floor.

Again the black shadowy life force was absorbed into the last brute carrying Alessandria.

The brute's grip tightened.

Nemesio stormed over.

He swirled and twirled his sword.

He needed to save Alessandria.

He wanted to slaughter this monster.

The brute whacked Nemesio in the stomach.

Nemesio collapsed to the floor. Holding his stomach.

Alessandria screamed as her bones compressed.

Hellen whacked the brute.

He didn't react.

Hellen whacked him again.

Still nothing.

Hellen jumped into the air.

Whacking the brute over the head.

This time he stopped. His gripped lightened on Alessandria. Not enough for her to move.

The brute spun.

Alessandria jerked.

Hellen whacked him a final time.

The brute grabbed the massive wooden stick with his teeth.

He crunched on it.

Snapping the massive wooden stick.

Hellen screamed in rage.

She charged.

The brute threw Alessandria to the ground.

The brute punched.

Hellen dodged it.

She slid under his legs.

She whacked his manhood with her hands.

The brute made a sound.

Alessandria wanted to help.

Her body wouldn't let her.

Hellen scratched the brute's back.

He seemed to be in pain.

Alessandria looked around. She needed to find a way to help.

Her body needed a few more minutes to recover.

Hellen screamed.

The brute grabbed her.

Hellen's hands waved to Alessandria.

Alessandria looked at the half-broken sword in

her hands.

She threw it.

Hellen caught it.

She slashed the brute's throat.

Blood gushed out of the wound.

The brute grabbed the half broken sword.

He thrusted it into Hellen.

The brute ripped it back out.

Alessandria's eyes widened.

The brute fell to the floor but so did Hellen.

Alessandria and Nemesio both found the strength to rush over.

Cradling Hellen in her arms, Alessandria opened Hellen's grey Procurator cloak to see a massive stab wound. An endless river of blood poured from the wound.

Hellen weakly stroked Alessandria's face.

Alessandria couldn't let Hellen die. She was her best friend. Her only true friend. This wasn't happening. It couldn't. Not Hellen. Maybe she could find a healer. Maybe she could-

Hellen placed a blood soaked finger on Alessandria's lips.

"Shhh, it's okay missy. I died protect ya. I always wanna die that way. Ma friend. Thank ya for everything. We had a great run me and you,"

She blew Alessandria a kiss.

Hellen turned to Nemesio.

"Ya protect her now. I'll haunt ya otherwise," Hellen said, laughing. Laughing until her face turned still.

CHAPTER 22

The air crackled and hummed loudly with bright red and dark blue magical energy.

I was really starting to get annoyed as these twenty hands held me tight. Feeling their disgusting breath on my skin was an assault on the senses. Their breath stunk of chemicals with hints of cinnamon and dried herbs.

The entire mob that was tightly packed into the throne room, with its blackening corrupted golden walls showing all sorts of mighty battles and long destroyed pieces of black silk sheets. The mob groaned and some of their skin cracked.

This ritual wasn't just about the Queen. Fateweaver was sucking the life force out of all of them.

My Father must have done some strong magic on me and my sister for Fateweaver to have to drain the lives of hundreds if not thousands. Just so he could kill us.

I hated this. I really hated this.

The fingers touching me made me want to scream and kill. I needed to feel their warm flesh under my talons. No, no, no I pushed the thoughts away not yet.

A part of me wondered if Alessandria was going to show up. I already had the love of my life injured on the floor with his nose bleeding.

A hurricane started overhead. The air screamed as the wind whipped around. The Queen turned deadly pale.

Lightning cracked and shot into the hearts of the mob.

The ritual had reached its climax.

The massive doors to the throne room exploded open.

Alessandria shouted something.

She was here.

I activated my Flesheater ability.

My eyes glazed over. Turning milky white.

My skin thickened into armour.

I smiled as my fingers and toes turned into razor sharp talons.

This time my skin transformed again. Millions of tiny metallic feathers covered them.

Fateweaver didn't seem to notice.

I slaughtered the men holding me.

They screamed.

My talons slashed into their flesh.

I loved the feeling of their warm beautiful flesh and blood covering my talons.

The mob was alert.

They were attacking.

Alessandria fought through the mob.

I spun.

I had to stop the ritual.

Fateweaver didn't notice us.

I shouted the Queen's name.

She reacted.

She chomped down on Fateweaver's tongue.

He gasped.

He screamed.

Blue fire cleansed the Queen's mouth.

Her eyes shot back to the present.

They were life filled once more.

Fateweaver snarled.

He whacked her with his staff.

I snarled.

The Queen rushed over to the remains of the throne.

She grabbed her glowing swords.

She charged into the mob.

It was going to be a beautiful slaughter.

I charged.

My talons chipped the floor.

Fateweaver braced.

I charged into him.

My talons slashing and lashing at him.

His staff took the impact.

My talons were powerful.

Fateweaver struggled to defend himself.

The staff crackled and hummed.

I chomped on the staff.

It tried to control me.

It pressed against my mind.

I let it in.

I flooded the staff with my desires for blood and

death.

I filled the staff with images of its death.

The staff shrieked.

The staff didn't want me.

I didn't care.

I clamped my fangs on it.

The staff cracked and exploded.

My fangs were intact.

Fateweaver panicked.

His wings swirled and twirled.

He flew into the air.

So did I.

His claws lashed at me.

Our claws and talons met.

Sparks flew off them.

We punched and kicked and scratched at each other.

Fateweaver shot fire out from his beak.

It hit me.

I burned.

I snarled. Falling to the ground.

My talons chipped the floor.

Red crimson burning symbols were all around me.

The ritual was still going on.

The Queen saw me.

Fateweaver tackled me.

I slammed my fists into his beak.

It cracked.

He fell off me.

I slashed a symbol.

The crimson flames died.

Fateweaver made a sound.

Maybe fear. Maybe a scream.

It was a sign.

The Queen slashed and lashed at the symbols.

Fateweaver went for her.

He flew past.

I grabbed Fateweaver's foot.

Throwing him against the blackened wall.

My talons sliced into his amazing flesh.

It was beautiful.

So much blood.

It was stunning.

Fateweaver kicked me hard.

My grip loosened.

He flew away.

Diving for the Queen.

I flew up.

Crashing into him.

I kept flying.

Slamming him into the ceiling.

My talons sliced up his face.

Bright blue feathers turned to ash.

He was dying.

His eyes widened.

A blast of magic made me let go.

I fell to the ground.

Mobsters spattered up my back as I landed.

Fateweaver flew at me.

His eyes widened.

The air around him screamed and crackled.

I spun to the Queen.

She thrusted her swords into the last symbol. The crimson flames died. Fateweaver fell to the ground.

It didn't take long for the rest of his bright blue feathers to turn to ash. Revealing a somewhat attractive young human man sitting on the floor. I didn't feel anything.

I didn't even care what magic he had used all this time. The human Fateweaver lacked all grandeur the magical one had. He was mortal. A pathetic human.

He looked up at all of us. Alessandria and Nemesio stood at my side with the Queen walking over to join us. She helped Harrison over. His hands were bloody and a dagger in his hand was dripping fresh blood.

I licked my lips but I knew my mission was done. Everyone was safe. I returned to my own mortal form.

Pointing a finger (not a talon) at the human Fateweaver, I looked at Alessandria. She didn't seem entirely sure what to do.

I took her sword. Ramming it through Fateweaver's skull. He turned to dust.

CHAPTER 23

Sitting down, Alessandria felt the smooth crushed velvet cover her back as she sat down on the posh, expensive chairs.

Alessandria didn't really want to be here. Especially, so late in the night but the Queen insisted and Alessandria wanted to serve her.

Her eyes narrowed as Alessandria saw the massive round brown oak table in front of her. It wasn't grand but it wasn't pointless either. It was more of a statement of friendship with a subtle reminder that Isabella was the Queen.

The smell of sweet orange incense filled her nose and Alessandria had to admit it was far better than the chemical smell with cinnamon and dried herbs from earlier.

Alessandria knew there was a large open window behind her and as the sounds from below reached her ears. She had to smile. The sounds of truly happy people laughing, singing and partying filled the air.

Everyone was celebrating their new freedom. Amazingly enough, some people had survived the mind control and thousands of citizens from the outer villagers had defeated Fateweaver's minions.

There were shouting and singing not about the church or Gods or Goddess. But of their Queen and the Firehearts. These people loved them all.

A part of Alessandria wasn't sure if she was happy to accept her new found popularity. But the people wanted it. The people loved her and her family. For the first time in decades, people actually liked the House of Fireheart. That made Alessandria smile.

What made Alessandria smile even more was seeing the amazing people around this table. Her family. Not by blood but of friendship and duty and love.

Looking straight ahead Alessandria looked at her Queen. You wouldn't know she had been mind controlled and had proven critical to defeating Fateweaver.

She didn't look weak or tired. Alessandria knew she was but the Queen didn't show it. The Queen's bright white silk robe and stunning youthful features were so clean, so young.

Even after everything she had been through, the Queen was still focused on her people.

Alessandria had to admire her for that. It was perhaps two, three hours since Daniel had slaughtered Fateweaver. (Alessandria was still surprised but happy it was all over) And the Queen had already gathered her few still living troops and set out a plan to make Ordericous strong again. Not for her and the nobility but for her people.

Turning her head, Alessandria looked at the amazing man who made the Queen's power and reach possible. Her soon-to-be brother in law. Harrison. Alessandria looked at him for a second or two. His longish blond hair was perfectly straight and he wasn't even dirty.

Of course Alessandria was curious where Daniel had found the brand new smooth wooden wheelchair Harrison sat on. But that wasn't a real thought.

She was just happy that Harrison was okay. He made her brother happy. Not easy to do and not easy to make him relax and enjoy life. Harrison allowed him to do that.

As much as she hated to admit it, Alessandria was concerned when Harrison was paralysed how that would affect him. She had seen so many friends in her military days get paralysed. Mostly they ended up killing themselves or becoming drunks.

Thankfully, Harrison was proof with the right support paralysed people could do amazing things. Maybe she would set up a charity to help those in need. Yes. She would.

Daniel kissed Harrison and Alessandria nodded to herself. Her brother was trapped in that throne room for ages with his Queen and the love of his life in danger. But he didn't seem phased. Daniel just sat there looking at Harrison. His eyes... happy and in love. A rare look for him.

His black leather trench coat and trousers a bit dirty. But Daniel did always prefer to be practical than be stylish. His dulled blade just there in his hand. Alessandria really smiled at that bit. Her brother was perfectly relaxed and at peace.

Looking at her beautiful Nemesio, admiring those beautiful eyes and that stunning blue and red fiery armour. Alessandria realised that she was at peace too.

She had almost everything she wanted. Her family was safe. Fateweaver was dead and she had Nemesio. Her stunning Nemesio.

But she didn't have everything. There was one more thing she needed.

"Friends, thank you. Thank you from the bottom of my heart," the Queen said. Her words still had her typically regal tone but she meant them.

Alessandria looked at Daniel. "Father would be proud of us,"

Daniel smiled.

"I am proud of all of you. You all stood by me these past months. You fought to defend me. Our enemies are dead. Thank you," the Queen said.

Daniel leaned forward. "Fateweaver, the Triad and the Orders are dead,"

Alessandria wasn't sure why he said those things but judging by the look on his face. Daniel couldn't believe it was all true.

"The Orders are dead?" Alessandria asked.

The Queen gestured her hand to her Regent Harrison.

"The Order of the Divine Air is wiped out. We destroyed the Order of the Sacred Fire. The other Orders fell under the mind control. Most were annihilated,"

"And the rest?" Nemesio asked.

"The three Sages came to me earlier," Harrison said, smiling. "They're dissolving themselves. They all said they saw the errors of the Inquisition. The homophobia, the racism and the zealous,"

Alessandria couldn't help but laugh. This was amazing. The Inquisition and the Church were gone. The two organisations that had made it hell for her family had dissolved themselves. Then Alessandria thought of something.

"What about the law Change?" she asked.

Harrison nodded. "They don't dissolve until you become coronated,"

Alessandria's eyes widened. She couldn't be coronated. She was not going to be Lady Fireheart. She was not going to be the head of the House of Fireheart. This was not happening.

Everyone must have seen Alessandria's face as Nemesio reached over and grabbed her hand.

Alessandria looked at Harrison. "Please Harrison. I'm begging you. Please call Court. I must change the law,"

Harrison gave Daniel a boyish grin.

Daniel kissed Harrison and turned to Alessandria. "It's already called. First light the Court will be in session,"

CHAPTER 24

Walking into the massive Court Chamber, I was surprisingly stunned. Sure I had seen paintings and heard about Court. But never have I ever seen it. It was amazing.

Looking from a large grey stone archway, I saw rows upon rows of brown oak seats that lined the three walls in front of me. They were tiered so no matter where someone was sitting. They could easily see the action.

But the seats did smell of harsh varnish and chemicals so it did make the chamber smell interesting.

Beautiful Harrison probably ordered a poor servant to varnish the seats to make them all good today.

Back in the day thousands of people would cramp into the chamber to see the decisions being made. I'm fairly sure this is the first time in about a century, Court's been called.

Looking straight ahead from me, an extremely shiny grey marble oval floor greeted me. It was rather seductive and it made me want to walk into the chamber further.

A part of me didn't want to. Not yet. In the middle of the Court Chamber was the famous massive oak oval table where all the decisions were made.

12 oversized black oak chairs were equally spaced around the table and they were already filled. The beautiful Queen sat proudly at the head of the table. Her sterile white silk dress was stunning but I (and everyone else here) knew she wanted to lure people into a false sense of security.

It had worked with Fateweaver. He didn't know how powerful she was in his mind prison.

All the other Heads or representatives of the Nobility were seated and talking amongst themselves. They probably hated me. I know we already had all their support. They swore their support on their honour, but I still felt uneasy.

What if they believed their honour wasn't as important as stopping me from becoming Lord Fireheart?

Looking around I just wanted to see a familiar face, a friend, an ally. It was just typical I saw Nemesio standing on an oak seat high in the tiers away from the oval table. He waved at me. I smiled back.

Seeing Alessandria in her perfectly clean black

leather armour, I saw her chatting and laughing with a random daughter of the Nobility. It made me smile to see her happy. I know she had had a lot on her plate over the past few months, so I was glad to see her enjoying herself.

Especially after Hellen's… death. I hugged Alessandria a lot when I heard the news. Hellen was a great girl. A great friend. We spend hours talking about the world, boys and other things. She loved hanging out with both of us but Alessandria was her favourite. I *felt* (more likely understood) why Alessandria was upset.

As much as I love autism and considering it a gift, it is times like this when I wished I was able to understand the feelings of others. I understood Hellen's death was sad and upsetting. But I couldn't *feel* it was sad and upsetting.

My dulled blade spun slowly in my hand, when me and my beautiful Harrison, or Lord Regent in this case, locked eyes. His beautiful perfect eyes were so life filled, so excited. He wanted this.

His longish blond hair was parted perfectly to the right and he looked stunning. I really wanted him but our wedding was later on. I guessed I had to keep my desires to myself for a little longer.

God, I loved that man.

Harrison stood up. "Lords, Ladies and everyone else. I welcome Master Daniel Fireheart to this meeting,"

Starting to walk over to the oval table, all eyes

turned to me, and Alessandria stood up and gestured I should take her seat.

I did.

Feeling the hard black oak pressed against my lower body and back, I still found it strange all the nobles and other representatives were smiling and looking at me.

Harrison gestured everyone to look at Alessandria.

"My fellow Nobles, I have bought you all here today for one purpose. We must change an unfair law-"

Multiple hands waved her silent. My eyes widened. Did these people really hate me so much they would sacrifice their honour to make sure I wasn't throned?

A large woman covered in thick metal armour with golden threads bonded to her head, clearly from the Order of the Precious Metal, stood up.

Alessandria and I both tensed. This couldn't be happening. We had her pledge. We had her seal.

The Sage of the Order of the Precious Metal gestured her hands around to the entire table.

"Lady Alessandria Fireheart, this is a waste of time," she said, her voice was well-aged, wise and demanding but a hint of fairness ran through it to.

My spirit sunk.

"I think, no I know I am speaking for all here. This man, this Fireheart man is a hero. He is a champion of what Ordericous should be. He risked everything to defend this country,"

Alessandria's jaw dropped. I couldn't blame her.

"Daniel Fireheart showed more intelligence than any man I have ever seen. He made sure Fateweaver was stalled long enough for help to arrive. He bought our Queen time. He bought Ordericous' time to survive. He is a hero,"

Harrison blew a kiss at me.

"And even when help arrived Daniel Fireheart did not cower in a corner and let others take over. He fought. He killed the foul Fateweaver. He saved our nation!"

Everyone nodded.

"So I speak for all of us here," the Sage turned to the Queen. "I am demanding you, your majesty. Change the law! Gays must be allowed to become Lords of Noble Houses,"

My eyes watered.

"I know Ordericous will be better off with Daniel Fireheart in charge of the House of Fireheart. I can think of no one I would rather see in power. He is a hero and I will happily serve him,"

The Sage knelt.

Everyone else stood up and knelt around me.

The Queen smiled and she knelt as well.

"Long live the Firehearts!" everyone shouted as one.

I couldn't believe it.

After a few seconds, everyone stood back up and took their seats. The Queen called for order and looked at me.

"Daniel Fireheart, you are a Master not no longer. From this moment forward, you are Lord Fireheart, Head of the House of Fireheart. And I decree any gay henceforth shall have the same opportunity as you,"

CHAPTER 25

The cold midday wind that smelt fresh and crisp blew past Alessandria, making the hairs on her neck stand up and her skin cold. This was the way it had to be.

Looking out over the valley miles away from the main city of Ordericous, Alessandria stared at the stunning valley. The rolling grass covered fields, the little houses of the farmers, the sheep and other animals eating away before it got too cold.

The ground felt hard and icy under Alessandria's feet but on top of the hill, it was a stunning view.

In the far distance, Alessandria could see the roaring waves crashing into the coast and Ordericous' main city was alive and well. That's all she ever wanted.

The wind continued to blow coldly over her skin as she looked out. Admiring the stunning natural beauty of the country she loved. Nemesio had asked to come with Alessandria to the hill top but

Alessandria needed to do this alone.

Turning around, Alessandria focused for a moment on the other side of the hill, it looked just as stunning and beautiful.

The sound of sheep, horses and other animals she couldn't quite identify echoed around the valley.

Then Alessandria looked down on the hard icy ground in front of her. The mount of freshly disrupted soil in the shape of a grave was there.

Alessandria just looked at the mount of dirt. It had taken a few hours to dig the grave herself and lovingly place the body in it.

Despite Alessandria not believing in any god or higher power, she still sprayed a bit of water on the grave. It wasn't holy but it was a silly little tradition.

At the top of the grave was the two broken halves of Hellen's massive wooden stick. It wouldn't seem right for her not to have it in death. Alessandria had buried Hellen in her grey Procurator cloak.

She hated this. Not because she was doing it alone. Daniel and Nemesio had really wanted to come with her to this tiny funeral. But Alessandria insisted it was what she needed.

Instead Alessandria hated this because she had lost her friend. Her best friend. Sure Hellen was a commoner, but Alessandria didn't care. Hellen was a great girl, a true friend and that's all that Alessandria needed.

For so long it was just Alessandria and Hellen, with Alessandria's Father dead, her Mother busy scheming and her brother… well that was her fault.

Hellen was there for Alessandria. She always was.

Alessandria thought about all the things they never got to do together. Like talk about kids, child rearing, their next case, their best and wrong investigations together. None of that would happen now.

Hellen never found a guy to marry or spend her life with. For some reason that scared or at least upset Alessandria, she knew Hellen loved her hook-ups and casual sex. But Alessandria knew she actually wanted a good guy to be with.

A part of Alessandria wished she could have done more for her friend. But in the end, Alessandria knew Hellen loved her for everything she did.

For starters Alessandria actually cared about her. Alessandria knew it was a sad truth in her friend's life that no one cared or loved her. Her Dominicus Procurator, a person who's meant to protect all the Procurators that serve under them, she didn't care. She thought Hellen was a sexual dinosaur who didn't deserve to be a Procurator.

When Alessandria had told the Queen's Dominicus Procurator about Hellen's heroic death. She laughed and called Alessandria a liar. Alessandria gave her a black eye, or two.

Her eyes watered now, Alessandria had lost so much recently. Her Mother and now her best friend.

But she knew she had gained a lot too. Her brother, a brother in law (soon) and her own stunning boyfriend.

Alessandria cocked her head. If anything she knew, she absolutely knew that Hellen would want Alessandria to be happy. And she was now. She had her Nemesio and she wasn't a Head of a Noble House.

Alessandria was still a Dominicus Procurator and she could and would continue to hunt down criminals and uphold the law.

Knowing she had a wedding to prepare for Alessandria looked down at the grave a final time.

"Good bye old friend,"

CHAPTER 26

Looking at myself in a large clean mirror, in a private yellow stone bed chamber the Queen had given to me so I could prepare for the wedding, my wedding, I stared at myself for a moment.

In the mirror, I looked at myself in my posh, expensive wedding suit with my shirt button undone and my dulled blade in my hand. Not moving. Just there.

The smell of sweet earthy aftershave filled the air and the taste of chocolate cake touched my tongue. I knew there was a little chocolate cake behind me on a stool from one of the cooks. I ignored it.

Bright orange light shone through a little round window high in the ceiling of the little room as the late afternoon sun started to set. The light gently warmed my neck.

I know the castle was in chaos but happy chaos. All the Nobility, former Inquisitors, the common folk, everyone was all preparing for my wedding.

I even heard a few servants rush past my room. It was all so surreal. I really didn't believe I was anyone special but here I was. A hero. A brother. A Lord. And soon a husband.

This was all so strange and alien to me. I didn't know how to feel, if I was able to feel too much. But I knew I was happy. I was happy for so many reasons.

My mind turned to what my Father would say and think (and my Mother) if they were here to see me. Of course, they would be proud. My parents would love me no matter what. But my Father would be especially proud because I defied all odds and ended a threat to the country.

My Mother naturally would be proud for a whole different reason. On the outside, she would be proud because I was doing tons of firsts and because I had made the House of Fireheart even more powerful.

On the inside though, she would be proud because I found something she could never have. Peace.

My Mother always pretended to be happy in her scheming, cunning plans but I knew she wasn't. It was all an act. Ever since my Father died she was different. Her mind was plagued by images of my Father, the man she was devoted to. The man who gave her so much. After all, she was just a piece of common filth in the beginning.

She would be proud I was happy.

A part of me wondered what I would be like if Harrison died or was taken from me. Then I remembered I didn't have to imagine. It had happened. My beautiful Harrison was taken from me by lies and deception.

But we had found each other again and that's what today was all about. My wedding. A symbol that everyone can be happy and in love.

So yes, my parents would be proud of me.

My mind turned to another topic- my Lordship. I was actually Head of a Noble House. In all honesty, I wasn't sure what I was more confused or shocked about. The fact the law was changed or that everyone demanded it.

Both were shocking. My entire life I was told I was a freak, a disgraceful person who was never, ever going to achieve anything.

I was bought up and experiencing a world that hated me. They all wanted me dead. I was an abomination, a freak or Unholy thing that needed to be slaughtered.

But in the end here I was. Standing in front of a mirror looking at a great man (if I do say so myself) in a wedding suit about to get married to the gay man I loved.

Most of all though, I was standing here. I was alive and loving life. All those homophobes or people who hated me for my autism were dead. The Church was physically killed. The Inquisition was mostly dead, but it was their ideology and faith that were dead.

So yes, I looked in the mirror and I saw a man

who was a survivor. A great supportive brother. A loyal servant to his Queen but most importantly a man who wanted to marry the love of his life and wanted to serve the people on Fireheart land to the best he possibly could.

That is the man I am.

CHAPTER 27

The perfect silk cushions made Alessandria's back feel like it was on a vacation. It was perfect.

As Alessandria sat in the front row on a very soft bench in the throne room, she couldn't be happier.

Looking around Alessandria couldn't believe the great work the Queen and her workers had done. They had scorched and cleansed the entire room of corruption and redecorated.

It was looked stunning and perfect for the wedding of the century.

The beautiful golden walls showing of their mighty depictions of grand battles and historical moments shone bright. Almost like they were cheering on and smiling at the wedding.

But Alessandria's favourite was a new addition. When her and Nemesio had attacked the throne room only yesterday she knew she saw the golden wall plain behind the throne.

Now it wasn't plain in the slightest. A massive

golden carving of Daniel and Harrison's faces were on the golden wall for the rest of Ordericous to see. Be it now or in ten thousand years they would see it. They should see this moment.

The gentle flapping of green, pink, red and dark blue sheets of silk hanging on the walls tied the throne room together. It was perfect.

Sounds of talking, laughing and being happy filled Alessandria's ears. This is what everyone needed.

Alessandria even laughed a little as she realised the massive heavy doors (and she knew they were heavy!) were wide open so the wedding could be heard through the castle.

Everyone from servants to commoners filled the castle just hoping to listen to the wedding. Maybe even see it!

Alessandria's nose wanted to protest as she smelt so many different perfumes and aftershaves that the nobility had worn. Some were fruity. Some were earthy. Lots smelt like cedarwood. But they were great.

A part of Alessandria wanted to think about the empty seats around her and her beautiful Nemesio. Hellen, her Mother and her Father weren't there.

As much as Alessandria wanted to swell on that fact. She knew it was selfish. This wasn't the time for that. This was a time for happiness and love. Her brother was getting married after all.

Looking forward, Alessandria couldn't help but

smile as she saw Daniel and Harrison up there together as one. Both in a stunning pair of expensive slightly shiny wedding suits.

They stared lovingly into each other's eyes and they smiled constantly at each other. That was love.

Alessandria took a deep breath as it felt like something was churning in her stomach. She ignored it.

Returning her attention to the two grooms, Alessandria nodded as the Queen in her golden silk dress wearing her heavy jewelled crown and holding her Sceptre looked at Alessandria.

Everyone fell silent. Nemesio grabbed Alessandria's hand.

The Queen gave everyone a massive smile.

"As Queen, I would normally give a speech or be posh about how brilliant this is and what a historic moment this is,"

Alessandria smiled. She liked where this was going.

"But I will not. As a friend, I want to say *Lord* Fireheart I am so pleased for you, and I wish you and Harrison a long happy marriage,"

The two grooms nodded their thanks.

"The rings please," the Queen said.

Alessandria completely forgot she had both rings in her hands. She gracefully walked over to the Queen and gave them to her.

As Alessandria sat back down the grooms did their vows. Said they loved each other no matter what and they were together forever. They mentioned their hardships and everything they had fought to get to this moment. It was beautiful.

Then they kissed.

Everyone erupted into a choir of cheers, congratulations and happiness. The entire room and castle had a buzz to it to.

Alessandria smiled and clapped her hands as she realised no one was faking this. Everyone in Ordericous wanted this wedding. They loved what Daniel had done for them.

Even Alessandria was a little surprised when some of that devotion was aimed towards her. When she was walking back from Hellen's grave earlier she had people chasing her asking for autographs.

The two beautiful grooms waved and walked down the aisle with their arms wrapped round each other's waist.

Everyone continued to cheer and congratulate them as they walked out the throne room. Followed by the Queen and everyone else followed them.

Nemesio went to get up but Alessandria didn't move. They were still holding hands so Nemesio couldn't move.

He looked at her. "What's wrong? This is great,"

Alessandria's smile was massive. "Of course this is amazing. I couldn't be happier,"

She gestured Nemesio to sit down.

"Nemesio, I love you. I really love you. I couldn't imagine life without you,"

He smiled. "I've been wanting to hear that for so long. And I've been wanting to say this for ages,"

Alessandria stroked his hand.

"Alessandria you are beautiful. The thought of losing you makes me scared. I really love you too. Will you..." Nemesio said, getting down on one knee.

Alessandria didn't let him finish his sentence. She kissed him. She really kissed him.

When Alessandria released him, she looked into his stunning eyes.

"Nemesio, I'm pregnant,"

Nemesio made a noise. Alessandria laughed at him. Nemesio kissed her hard.

"You're happy then?" Alessandria asked.

"Of course. You're going to be an amazing mum. It's going to be great. I can teach them sports-"

Alessandria kissed him again.

As they got up hand in hand walking off to the wedding reception, Alessandria knew her life was complete. She had everything she ever wanted and as she walked with Nemesio. Alessandria finally found what love felt like- amazing, confusing and it made you feel as light as a feather.

AUTHOR'S NOTE

Wow!

A massive, massive thank you from me for reading this great page-turning book and series.

I have truly loved writing this great series. It's been great to see the characters develop, the relationships and the plot.

At the time of writing in July 2021, this has been my favourite series to write. I've had tons of fun with these characters, and I really hope you have to.

In terms of this book, it was always about bringing together all the various plot threads and tying things up in the series.

From Fateweaver to the Triad to the law change and the relationships in the book, I wanted to tie it all up in this book.

However, I also wanted to give these characters some twists and turns to finish up their character journeys. The main one of course being Daniel's as he needed to buy time for Alessandria to destroy the

Loom and come to the rescue.

It was only when Alessandria turned up so she could possibly calm him down if the Flesheater ability acted up that he activated it and saved Ordericous.

In addition, I really wanted to prove and explore a few things with this series and book in particular. The biggest of these being autism and I wanted to explore the difficulties and gifts autism gives people in a positive light.

My background is in clinical (mental health) psychology so I know mental conditions are seen in a positive light. Where autism, depression, anxiety and more aren't seen in a negative light. They aren't diseases that destroy lives. Sure there are difficulties but when seen in a positive light with the right support provided, people with mental conditions can thrive.

Granted I just gave you a grossly oversimplified crash course in clinical psychology. But this is what I wanted to show in this series right from the start.

Because we see Daniel Fireheart, a gay autistic man, who tried to kill himself because of the difficulties autism gave him and the lies.

But we also see him thrive with the support of Alessandria and Harrison to become a hero to his country. Without his autism none of this would have been possible. As showed in *Heart of Bones* were Fateweaver Primus tried to control him, but she revealed to Daniel she couldn't control his mind because of his autism.

So all in all, the message (if there was one) of the series is to celebrate life and accept people's differences and just because someone is autistic and paralysed doesn't mean they can't do things in life.

I've absolutely loved writing these books and thank you for reading. I really do appreciate it.

Have a great day and I hope to see you in another book soon!

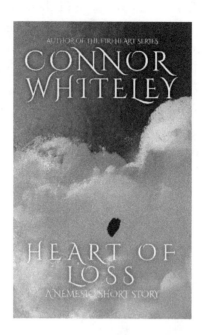

GET YOUR FREE AND EXCLUSIVE
SHORT STORY NOW! LEARN ABOUT
NEMESIO'S PAST!

https://www.subscribepage.com/fireheart

Thank you for reading.

I hoped you enjoyed it.

If you want a FREE book and keep up to date about new books and projects. Then please sign up for my newsletter at www.connorwhiteley.net/

Have a great day.

CHECK OUT THE PSYCHOLOGY WORLD PODCAST FOR MORE PSYCHOLOGY INFORMATION!

AVAILABLE ON ALL MAJOR PODCAST APPS.

About the author:

Connor Whiteley is the author of over 30 books in the sci-fi fantasy, nonfiction psychology and books for writer's genre and he is a Human Branding Speaker and Consultant.

He is a passionate Warhammer 40,000 reader, psychology student and author.

Who narrates his own audiobooks and he hosts The Psychology World Podcast.

All whilst studying Psychology at the University of Kent, England.

Also, he was a former Explorer Scout where he gave a speech to the Maltese President in August 2018 and he attended Prince Charles' 70th Birthday Party at Buckingham Palace in May 2018.

Plus, he is a self-confessed coffee lover!

OTHER SHORT STORIES BY CONNOR WHITELEY

Blade of The Emperor

Arbiter's Truth

The Bloodied Rose

Asmodia's Wrath

Heart of A Killer

Emissary of Blood

Computation of Battle

Old One's Wrath

Other books by Connor Whiteley:

The Fireheart Fantasy Series

Heart of Fire

Heart of Lies

Heart of Prophecy

Heart of Bones

Heart of Fate

The Garro Series- Fantasy/Sci-fi

GARRO: GALAXY'S END

GARRO: RISE OF THE ORDER

GARRO: END TIMES

GARRO: SHORT STORIES

GARRO: COLLECTION

GARRO: HERESY

GARRO: FAITHLESS

GARRO: DESTROYER OF WORLDS

GARRO: COLLECTIONS BOOK 4-6

GARRO: MISTRESS OF BLOOD

GARRO: BEACON OF HOPE

GARRO: END OF DAYS

Winter Series- Fantasy Trilogy Books

WINTER'S COMING

WINTER'S HUNT

WINTER'S REVENGE

WINTER'S DISSENSION

Miscellaneous:

THE ANGEL OF RETURN

THE ANGEL OF FREEDOM

All books in 'An Introductory Series':

BIOLOGICAL PSYCHOLOGY 3RD EDITION

COGNITIVE PSYCHOLOGY THIRD EDITION

SOCIAL PSYCHOLOGY- 3RD EDITION

ABNORMAL PSYCHOLOGY 3RD EDITION

PSYCHOLOGY OF RELATIONSHIPS- 3RD EDITION

DEVELOPMENTAL PSYCHOLOGY 3RD EDITION

HEALTH PSYCHOLOGY

RESEARCH IN PSYCHOLOGY

A GUIDE TO MENTAL HEALTH AND TREATMENT AROUND THE WORLD- A GLOBAL LOOK AT DEPRESSION

FORENSIC PSYCHOLOGY

THE FORENSIC PSYCHOLOGY OF
THEFT, BURGLARY AND OTHER
CRIMES AGAINST PROPERTY

CRIMINAL PROFILING: A FORENSIC
PSYCHOLOGY GUIDE TO FBI
PROFILING AND GEOGRAPHICAL
AND STATISTICAL PROFILING.

CLINICAL PSYCHOLOGY

FORMULATION IN PSYCHOTHERAPY

PERSONALITY PSYCHOLOGY AND
INDIVIDUAL DIFFERENCES

CLINICAL PSYCHOLOGY
REFLECTIONS VOLUME 1

CLINICAL PSYCHOLOGY
REFLECTIONS VOLUME 2

CPSIA information can be obtained
at www.ICGtesting.com
Printed in the USA
LVHW082301181021
700771LV00002B/632